The Heaven Shop

The Heaven Shop

Deborah Ellis

Fitzhenry & Whiteside

Published in Canada by Fitzhenry & Whiteside,
195 Allstate Parkway, Markham, Ontario L3R 4T8

Published in the United States by Fitzhenry & Whiteside,
121 Harvard Avenue, Suite 2, Allston, Massachusetts 02134

www.fitzhenry.ca   godwit@fitzhenry.ca

10 9 8 7 6 5 4 3 2 1

National Library of Canada Cataloguing in Publication

Ellis, Deborah, 1960-
    The heaven shop / Deborah Ellis.
ISBN 1-55041-908-0, Hardcover
ISBN 1-55041-907-2, Softcover
    I. Title.
PS8559.L5494H42 2004   jC813'.54   C2004-901913-9

U.S. Publisher Cataloging-in-Publication Data
(Library of Congress Standards)

Ellis, Deborah.
    The heaven shop/ Deborah Ellis.—1st ed.
[250] p. : cm.
Summary: Binti and her siblings are orphaned when their father dies of
AIDS. Split up and sent to relatives all over Malawi, they suffer increasing
hardship until they are reunited through the influence of their formidable
grandmother.

ISBN 1-55041-908-0, Hardcover
ISBN 1-55041-907-2, Softcover
1. AIDS (Disease)—Fiction—Juvenile literature. 2. Grandmothers—
Fiction – Juvenile literature. I. Title.
[Fic] dc22 PZ7.E655He 2004

Fitzhenry & Whiteside acknowledges with thanks the Canada Council
for the Arts, the Government of Canada through the Book Publishing
Industry Development Program (BPIDP), and the Ontario Arts Council
for their support of our publishing program.

Design by Fortunato Design Inc.
Cover illustration by Janet Wilson
Author's photo by John Spray

Printed in Canada

Acknowledgements

To the children left behind
Deborah Ellis

I'd like to acknowledge Pamela Brooke of the Story Project in Malawi, for sharing her house and her wine, and introducing me to the children on the radio; Mary Phiri of Friends of Mulanje Orphans, for showing me their amazing work; Laura Peetoom, a wonderful editor; and my father Keith Ellis and Dawn Dowling, for their e-mails, which kept me company when I was traveling. And special thanks to the incredible people of Malawi and Zambia, for their hospitality, and their willingness to share their stories.

Chapter One

"YOUR MOTHER DIED OF AIDS!"

"She did not!"

"She did, too. Everyone knows it."

"She died. She just died. She didn't have AIDS."

"She was a bad woman and she died of AIDS and ..."

"Cut!"

Binti was so caught up in the scene that she kept saying her lines, and Mr. Wajiru had to give the direction again.

"Cut! Binti, you are not holding yourself at the proper distance from the microphone. We will have to start the scene from the top."

Binti frowned at Stewart, the other child in the cast. He was beaming.

Go ahead and smile, Binti thought. Your part is so easy a chicken could play it.

"As for the rest of you," the director continued, "you could all take a lesson from the way Binti was reading that scene. She sounded like an actual person. Now, if she could just sound like an actual person into her microphone."

The cast took advantage of the short break in the taping to clear their throats, shuffle papers, blow their noses, and give themselves a stretch. While the tape was rolling, no one could move a muscle, as every little sound would be picked up by the microphones. Although this was only a rehearsal into the mikes, and they wouldn't be recording until after the next break, Mr. Wajiru insisted they behave as if they were taping.

"All right. Get ready. We'll take that piece from the beginning."

Binti took a deep breath to relax herself and to help her focus. She knew her lines and everyone else's lines, so she didn't need the script that was propped up on the stand in front of her.

She looked across the little room that was the Story Time studio. Blankets hung on the walls to keep their voices from echoing on the cement and sounding funny on the radio. The only ornament was a drawing of a bird Binti's brother Kwasi had done. Mr. Wajiru kept it in the studio to remind them that their voices soared over Malawi.

In Binti's mind, the studio walls turned into Gogo's house, where most of the action in the show, "Gogo's Family," took place. Binti played Kettie, Gogo's granddaughter. In her mind, Stewart stopped being an annoying cast mate and turned into the cousin Binti's character didn't like, who had come to live in Gogo's house because of his mother's death. When the director's order to begin came through the loudspeaker, Binti was ready.

"Thank you. That was very good," Mr. Wajiru said at the end of the scene. "We will now take a break. Refresh yourselves. Come back ready to record."

Binti felt drained, like a big part of her had been poured into the microphone. She'd get her energy back during the break. She always did.

"Binti, the journalist from the Youth Times is here to interview you," Miss Jimu, the production assistant, put her hand on Binti's shoulder to get her attention.

Binti hadn't forgotten. She followed Miss Jimu into one of the little offices. A young woman wearing trousers was sitting among the stacks of paper.

"This is Binti Phiri," Miss Jimu said, then left the two of them alone.

The reporter smiled and shook Binti's hand. "Thank you for making the time to meet with me."

Binti moved some files off a chair and onto the floor so she could sit down. She had a hard time taking her eyes off the clothes the reporter was wearing. The reporter noticed, and laughed. "It's been many years since President-for-Life Banda was in power, but people are still surprised to see a woman wearing trousers."

Binti knew that, under President Banda, it was against the law for women and girls to wear anything but long skirts and dresses. She, herself, had never worn trousers. She had dresses for every day, dresses for special occasions, and, of course, her school uniform, which had a skirt. She always wore her second-best dress to the tapings. It was blue with lace that Junie had sewn on. Her best dress was reserved for church. "Some of my father's customers say life in Malawi was better under President Banda. More people had jobs."

"More people were tortured, too, for voicing their opinions. Which do you think is more important, Binti—jobs or free speech?"

Binti thought for a moment. "It depends on how poor you are."

The reporter laughed but in a good way, not at Binti. "Now, I know you don't have a lot of time, so why don't we begin? I have a fact sheet that gives me some basic information on you. I know you are in standard seven at St. Stephen's School for Girls. You are thirteen years old, and your role on 'Gogo's Family' is your first professional acting job. That leaves a lot of questions for me to ask. To start with, who else is in your family?"

"My older sister, Junie, is sixteen. All she can think about is Noel, her boyfriend. They're engaged to be married, but my father is making Junie finish school first. Well, Junie would do that, anyway. She gets good grades.

"Next is my brother, Kwasi. He's fourteen. He

likes to draw, mostly birds, but he's good at drawing people, too." She didn't add that his shy, lop-sided smile usually meant he was thinking about what he would like to draw. "I'm next, and I'm the youngest."

"And your parents?"

"There's just my father. My mother died six years ago, of an illness." The reporter didn't ask what type of illness. Binti didn't know. She remembered only that her mother stayed in bed a lot, getting smaller and smaller until she just seemed to fade away. Then, one day, the house was full of relatives, and Mama was gone for good.

"What work does your father do?"

"He runs a small business. He makes and sells coffins. His shop is called Heaven Shop Coffins, and is along New Chileka Road. We live in back of the shop." Binti hoped the reporter would print that part in the paper, although her father didn't really need new business. He always had lots of orders to fill. "He's teaching carpentry to my brother and me, but we're not very good yet. I'm better than my brother, though. He doesn't like to take the time to measure properly."

"Do you have a Gogo in your real life?" Gogo was what most Malawians called their grandmothers.

"I never met my mother's mother. My father's mother lives in Mulanje. She is the person I call Gogo. I don't know her very well, though."

Binti didn't add that she didn't know Gogo at all,

that Gogo last came to Blantyre when Mama died. She hadn't stayed long, but her hug was kind.

"'Gogo's Family' is the most popular radio show in Malawi," the reporter said. "Your voice is heard by millions of people every week, in homes and villages all over the country. I understand you get fan mail."

"I get lots of letters, from children and from grownups."

"And what do the letters say?"

Binti grinned. "A lot of them tell me I'm being horrible. They think they are writing to Kettie, my character. The ones who write to me, Binti, say nice things, or they write about how something similar happened to them."

"Are you like Kettie?"

"I'm much nicer," Binti said. "Mr. Wajiru says my character is so awful because she teaches people how not to be."

"How does it feel to be so famous?"

"It's a team effort," she said, which was one of the answers she'd discussed with the director, who had rehearsed the interview with her. "And it makes my father proud," she added, with another smile.

Binti watched the reporter scribble down what she'd said. She hadn't really answered the question. How *did* she feel? She liked the money she got each week. Even though most of it went into the family pot, she, Junie, and Kwasi were also given pocket money from it. She liked coming into the Story Time house and being given a handful of fan mail, although she didn't like the work it took to answer the letters. She liked feeling special when she walked through the markets of Blantyre. Even though people in the shops and stalls didn't know who she was by looking at her, her voice would have come into their homes.

Mostly what she liked, though, were taping days, being part of the cast, and working hard at something that was so much fun. Even though she often had to say a line over and over to get it right, getting it right in the end was worth the work.

The reporter scribbled away, then looked back at her notes. "I forgot to ask how you got the job."

"There was an audition," Binti said. "My father saw a notice up on the bulletin board in the library. My sister, Junie, brought me here. There was a long line-up of kids. We each had to read something in front of a group of adults. Some of us were asked to do it again. I kept reading until I was the only one left, and they gave me the job."

"And you have been with the show for four months?"

"Eight," Binti corrected. "We've been on the air for four months, but we tape four months in advance."

"The show deals with serious issues, like AIDS, crime, people losing their jobs. Do you always under- stand what is being talked about?"

Of course I understand! Binti wanted to say. I'm very smart, or I wouldn't have gotten the job. But she didn't say that. She didn't want the newspaper readers to think she thought too much of herself. "I try to act like a regular child would. In the show we are doing today, I make fun of a cousin who comes to live in our house. I don't want him to be there, so I try to make him feel bad by saying his mother died of AIDS. My character wants to make him feel ashamed. Kids will say things like that."

"How is everything going in here?" Mr. Wajiru burst into the room with his usual whoosh of energy. "Binti, if you need to do anything before we start recording, you should go and do it now."

Mr. Wajiru wouldn't let anyone interrupt the recording for things they should have taken care of on a break.

"You have enough for your article, don't you?" Mr. Wajiru asked the reporter. The reporter looked like she was going to say no, but Mr. Wajiru swept right on. "Go out to the front office. They will give you some papers that will explain all we are doing here. We don't just produce a radio show, you know. We also publish comic books on HIV/AIDS, on nutrition, on all sorts of things."

The director swept away the reporter with one arm, and swept Binti off in the direction of the studio with the other. Mr. Wajiru always wore colorful clothing, which added to the drama of his gestures. Today, he was wearing a bright green and orange loose pullover shirt with wide sleeves.

Ten minutes later, Binti, feeling fresh and energized, was back in front of her microphone.

"Is everybody here?" The director looked around as he strode into the studio. "Everyone in position? Good. Let's produce something that Malawi will find worth listening to."

He said that at the beginning of every taping. Binti liked to hear it. She liked to think that they were doing good work, something that people would want to hear. As always at the beginning of taping, a bolt of excitement surged through her.

The director left the microphone room. Binti watched him through the large glass window as he took his place beside the technician at the sound board with all the buttons on it. Binti could tell he was excited, too.

She must have been smiling at him, because he caught her eye, then, and smiled right back. But only for a moment.

In the next instant, he was barking, "All right, everyone get ready. We are going to begin. Act one, scene one. And try to sound like real people!"

The radio play began. Binti stopped being Binti and became Kettie, the youngest child in Gogo's family.

Chapter Two

WHEN THE TAPING WAS OVER, Binti received the script for next week's show. She stayed around as long as the staff would let her, sipping juice and hanging on to that special feeling she got on taping day.

Binti was allowed to travel to and from the radio house by herself. She had enough money on her to take a minibus, but she preferred walking. The minibusses were always scrunched-in crowded, and it was impossible to feel special when she was squished in.

At the edge of the property, Binti looked back briefly at the radio house before walking through the gate. It really was a house, with gray brick walls and a red tile roof, set back from the road in a garden with flowers and trees. The street it was on was cool, shady and modern.

"Someday, I'll live in a house just like it," she said to herself, before nodding to the guard to have him open the gate. Like all fancy houses, this one had a high wall around it and guards to keep away thieves.

Binti made sure the script she carried faced outward, so people who could read would be able to read the title, and see that she was important. Then she headed for home.

Binti loved living in Blantyre, Malawi's largest city. It was named after the city in Scotland where David Livingstone was born. He was a *mzunga*, a white person, who came to Malawi in the 1800s, when it was still called Nyasaland. Blantyre was a busy city, with paved streets and fancy bank buildings. Binti loved the excitement of being around all the shops, even though she wasn't as big on shopping as Junie was. And Blantyre was in a high part of Malawi, so along with all the shops there were hills and beautiful places to look at. There was even a small mountain, Mount Soche.

Binti passed the fancy hotel, called the Mount Soche Hotel, after the mountain. In one of the trees in the garden, Binti spotted the little red bee-eater birds her brother liked to draw. Many important events were held in the big lounge inside the hotel. Story Time held a party there when the radio show began. Binti and her family got to attend. It was fun and exciting but so different from her regular life, it was almost a relief to go home to the coffin shop.

Now, Binti would find a party like that a lot easier. She hoped there would be another one soon.

Binti turned off the main street, going down the dirt lane that went by the library, passing the children selling sweets off up-turned cardboard boxes. She was sweating as she walked; even though it was early May, and Malawi was moving into winter, the afternoon was still warm. Binti stood at one of the library windows. The library was full of people who didn't have time to read during the work week. Her sister, Junie, was supposed to be in there, studying.

Binti spotted her sister, sitting at a table across from her boyfriend, Noel. They were studying each other much more than their books. Binti raised a hand to rap on the window, but was stopped by something she saw in Junie's face.

Junie had an oval face, like their father's. Binti's was more round, like their mother's. Looking at Junie, Binti saw a flash of something she'd seen long, long ago—her father looking at her mother, so crazy in love that tenderness and pain and all the hope in the world was in that one look.

Binti dropped her hand. There was more in that look than she wanted to think about on taping day.

She headed toward home. She was soon on New Chilika Road, where her house was. On one side of this road, the secondhand clothing dealers had set themselves up in stalls of wooden poles roped and hammered together, or on sheets of plastic spread on the ground. The jeans, shirts, dresses, and sweaters that people in America no longer wanted were piled in huge stacks. The late Saturday afternoon crowd was thick among the clothing stalls. When Junie wasn't with Noel, she was often looking through the stalls.

She had an eye for being able to spot something great in the middle of a large pile of ugly things.

On the other side of the street, small businesses crowded into every inch of spare ground, leaving a narrow footpath for pedestrians. Behind them the land sloped into a small valley with homes and paths leading to other parts of Blantyre.

Binti walked by the fruit and vegetable sellers. Some had proper stalls. Most were women sitting beside their displays of bananas or tomatoes. Boys cut up potatoes for frying. Others walked around, carrying the shirts or pens or batteries they wanted people to buy.

Binti saw something that made her stop suddenly on the path, bringing complaints from the woman walking behind her. Binti stepped to the side to let the woman pass.

She was standing in front of a new coffin shop.

My father won't like this, she thought. I don't like this. It will take away from his business. Her father talked to her about things that affected how much money the business made, like the price of wood, and competition.

She stepped off the path and into the new coffin shop's yard. This shop looked a lot like her father's, except that the coffin leaning against the wall was not plain wood but a beautiful green material. Binti went up for a closer look.

"It's beautiful, isn't it?" a man asked her. He was

not covered in wood dust the way her father often was. "My name is Mr. Tsaka. This is my business."

Binti said hello politely, and admitted that the coffin was beautiful.

"But surely you are not here to buy a coffin," Mr. Tsaka said.

"I just wanted to see what it was made of."

Some grownups came into the yard. Mr. Tsaka put on the face that shopkeepers keep for customers. Binti's father had that face, too, but only used it when he was too tired to smile naturally. "Well, now you have seen, so go on home. People will not buy my coffins if they see a child here. They will think this is not a serious place."

Binti craned her neck to see what was in the back of the shop. She saw more fancy coffins, wrapped in clear plastic. She wanted to look closer, but she didn't think the owner would let her. She went on her way.

Before long, she could see the sign for her father's business. HEAVEN SHOP COFFINS—*Our Coffins Will Take You Quickly to Heaven*.

Binti was home.

Her brother, Kwasi, was sitting on the ground, his back against the signpost, wearing his lop-sided smile, making a drawing of their father as he worked. "My fingers get hungry to draw," he sometimes said. Binti bent down to look at the sketch. It was done in plain pencil, not the colored ones Kwasi sometimes used. He had a small watercolor paint set, too, that he got for Christmas last year. It was too precious for him to use very often.

"That's good," she said. "You've made him look too skinny, though." In Kwasi's drawing, her father's clothes hung off him. His arms were like sticks, and his face was all bones.

"He *is* really skinny," Kwasi said.

"Not *that* skinny. And you'd better slip some cardboard under your seat if you don't want Junie to nag you about dirt on your trousers."

"You're in my light," Kwasi told her, which was what he always said when he wanted someone to go away.

The coffin shop's workbench was in the middle of the yard, open on all sides, with a roof of tin sheeting. Binti's father was standing at the workbench, measuring a board. Binti noticed, with a start, that his arm was thinner than the board.

"Hi, Bambo," Binti said, greeting her father in the Malawian way.

He looked up and smiled. "How's my famous daughter today?" His eyes had their usual sparkle.

"Oh, Bambo," Binti complained, but she smiled, too. "You're going to be famous soon, too. I told the reporter all about Heaven Shop Coffins."

"Oh, yes, you had that newspaper interview today, didn't you?"

"Soon you'll have people coming from all over Malawi to buy your coffins."

"Perhaps I will have to grow another pair of arms," her father joked. "Then I will be able to saw wood with one pair, and join it together with the other."

"We'd have to get you new shirts," Binti said. "If shirts with four sleeves exist, Junie will find them."

"You will hang up that good dress now and make sure your clothes are ready for church tomorrow," he said. "Then perhaps you could make your old father a cup of tea."

"I think I could do that." It was a regular thing to do when she got back from the studio. She went through the covered part of the yard, where the wooden coffins were stacked up out of the rain, and into the little house at the back. She put the tea-kettle on the stove, and by the time the water was boiled, she had changed out of her good dress into an old skirt and shirt.

She put her radio money away in the old sugar bowl on the high shelf, then made three cups of tea. Kwasi came inside for his cup. Binti took the other two outside for her and her father.

Her father took the tea and blew on it, to cool it a bit before sipping on it.

"I saw Junie in the library, making cow-eyes at Noel."

"As long as she makes cow-eyes at her books, too," Bambo said. Junie was due to take her final school-leaving exam in less than a year. If she got a good result, she could go to university, after working for a while to make some money.

"She goes all stupid when she's with him."

"Love makes us all stupid," her father said. "Sometimes, I would look at your mother and forget everything, even my own name." He put his tea to one side, and went to lift another board onto his worktable. His energy seemed to give way before the board was up, and it fell to the ground. Binti helped him raise it up again.

"Are you getting sick again, Bambo? Do you want me to hold the board for you?"

"I am not getting sick, and I would like you to do your job and sweep the yard," he told her.

Binti picked up the broom. Her father liked a clean shop.

"We must do all we can to show respect for our customers and their grief," he often said. "A messy shop tells them their grief is not important to us, and they will go somewhere else to buy their coffins."

Also, a clean shop cut down the risk of fire. Binti carefully swept the wood chips away, and smoothed out the dirt in the yard. She left the wood chips in a tidy pile on the edge of the yard. Someone who needed fuel and didn't have any money would come and get them during the night.

"There is a new coffin shop opening up down the road," she said. "They have some very fancy coffins on display."

"I went down to that shop when you were at the radio house today," her father said, sanding off a rough edge of the board. "I wanted to welcome them to the neighborhood. Unfortunately, there is plenty of business for us both. Those fancy coffins they have come in pieces from South Africa. All they have to do is screw the pieces together. Where is the craft in that? The coffins are beautiful, but they are not for us."

Binti knew he was talking to himself as much as he was talking to her. She watched him expertly cut the joints that fit the boards together, without nails. He used very few nails, but his coffins had never come apart.

"That's why so many families come back to us," he said often.

Binti imagined how awful it would be if a coffin fell apart during a funeral. Then she noticed a child coming into the yard.

"I need a coffin for my puppy." The little boy cradled a small animal in his arms, nestled against the picture of Mickey Mouse on his torn t-shirt.

Her father stopped his sawing, came around the worktable, and knelt down in front of the boy. "Your puppy has died. That's very sad. What was his name?"

"Mandela," the boy whispered, a tear running down his cheek.

"A noble name. We must make him a noble coffin." He straightened up, using his workbench to support him as he rose. "Binti, see what lumber pieces we have."

Binti ran to the scrap lumber pile. This was for the odds and ends of lumber too small for even baby coffins. She picked out some pieces.

"These will do very nicely," Bambo said. "Do this with me, Binti. Let's see how good you are getting."

Binti was a lot slower than her father, and her joints were not as tight, but before long, the two of them had the small coffin cut and put together. "You're getting to be a good carpenter," her father said. "Will this do?" he asked the boy.

The boy gently put the puppy into the box. "He'll be cold."

"Binti, fetch one of my nice clean handkerchiefs." Binti knew just where he kept them, since she usually folded them and put them away after Junie had done the laundry. She fetched him one. He tucked it around the puppy, then put the tiny lid on the coffin.

"How much does it cost?" the boy asked.

"Do you have any money?"

The boy shook his head.

"I didn't think you did. Take the little coffin today, but come back tomorrow to help tidy my work area. I help you, and you help me. Is that a bargain?"

The little boy solemnly nodded, and shook Bambo's hand. Then he hugged the tiny coffin in both arms, and left the coffin yard. Binti and her father watched him go.

"By tomorrow he will have forgotten," Binti said.

"You're wrong. He'll be back. We made a bargain."

"I hope that doesn't start other kids bringing dead animals here for a free coffin," Binti said. "They could even get a dead rat from a rubbish heap, say it was a pet, get a free wooden box, and toss the rat back on the tip."

"I think we can manage to make a few free coffins for pets if we have to," her father said, "as long as the pets aren't too big. I draw the line at free coffins for hippos."

Binti giggled. She'd seen hippos at Lake Malawi when they'd gone to visit their uncle once in Monkey Bay, years ago. They were huge, funny-looking, and had nasty tempers. They'd make terrible pets. "Or an elephant!"

"Or a giraffe! Can you imagine the shape of a coffin I'd have to make for a pet giraffe?" Her father drew a series of angles in the air with his finger. The two of them bent over with laughter.

Then a pickup truck full of crying and singing women pulled up, and it was time to stop laughing and get back to work.

Chapter Three

"WHY ARE YOU IN SUCH A BAD MOOD this morning?" Binti asked Junie as they walked to school a few weeks later. Junie had been frowning and trying to get their father into an argument ever since Binti got out of bed. If Bambo had noticed, he hadn't given any sign of it, which amused Binti and Kwasi but hadn't done anything to improve Junie's mood.

They walked in silence for most of the trip. Their school uniforms looked sharp on both of them, but on Junie, as with everything she wore, it also looked chic and elegant. Binti couldn't figure out how she did it.

"What's bothering you?"

Junie was ready to talk. "I got up early to do the books." Junie kept the accounts for the coffin business. She made Binti help her sometimes, as training. Binti would have to do the books when Junie got married.

"Was there something wrong?"

"There was a lot less money than there should have been. Bambo has given most of the profits from last month to the cousins."

Binti didn't say anything. She knew what was coming.

"Any time we start to get ahead, he sends money off to the cousins. I know they're family, but how much money do they need?"

Still, Binti said nothing.

"I asked Bambo about it this morning when I made his breakfast," Junie said.

"And?"

"And he said what he always said. 'Don't you have food on your plate? Don't you sleep under a roof?' That's not everything, I'm going to say to him one of these days. There's more to life than just eating and sleeping. There's thinking about the future, and planning for it."

"Is there something you need?" Binti asked. "I'm earning money."

"Don't start talking to me about what a big star you are. This isn't about you."

"I only said …"

"You're just a child. You think that because today is wonderful, tomorrow will be wonderful, too. But it doesn't always work that way. Things go wrong. People get sick. We should be planning for when things don't go well. We should be putting money aside. That's what I learned in business class, but he gives it all away. 'Family,' he says, but what are we?"

"Why wouldn't things go well?" Binti asked.

"Oh, you're such a child." Junie started to walk faster. Binti tried to keep up with her, but Junie didn't want that. "Back off, or you'll be in such trouble!" she snapped. Her anger pumped her legs until she was far ahead of Binti.

Junie was always telling Binti she'd be in such trouble for something. It annoyed Binti more each time she heard it. And it was just one of many bossy, annoying ways Junie had. Like this morning: Junie had told her to wear her sweater to school. "It's chiperoni season," she'd said. The chiperoni was the cold wind that blew around Malawi in the winter months of June, July and August. Binti knew as well as Junie that it was winter, and she liked the light blue sweater that went with her school uniform of navy skirt, white blouse, and navy blazer. In fact, she had been about to go back inside to fetch it when Junie had ordered her to put it on.

"Don't wear it, then," Junie had said, when Binti glared at her and slammed the door, "but don't complain when you catch a cold and lose your voice and can't go on the radio."

Binti should have given in at that point, but she wanted to prove that she was as stubborn as Junie. Later that morning, shivering on stage in the school Assembly Hall, she felt more foolish than victorious.

Mrs. Chintu, the Headmistress, climbed the steps to the platform. "Good morning, girls," she said.

"Good morning, Headmistress." Binti and the other prefects rose to their feet, then gave the traditional respectful curtsey. The prefects were the students chosen to help keep order in the school. Mrs. Chintu wanted all of them, except the ones on duty patrolling the assembly hall, to be onstage with her during the morning assembly.

Mrs. Chintu stopped in front of Binti. "Why are you shivering?" she asked. "Malaria?"

"Chiperoni," Binti answered.

Mrs. Chintu lost all sympathy. "You should have worn a sweater. You may borrow one from the clothes box in the office. You can't concentrate on your lessons when you are cold."

Binti didn't want to touch the clothes box, which was full of things donated by the families of wealthy students and British donors for students who were on scholarship. They weren't uniform, and anyone wearing a charity sweater stood out like a *mzunga*. But no one ever said no to the Headmistress. Mrs. Chintu would remember and would come to Binti's classroom to check.

"Yes, ma'am," said Binti.

St. Peter's was one of the best schools for girls in Blantyre. It was a very old school, built originally by the Presbyterian Church people who came to Malawi from Scotland. For a long time, all the Headmistresses had been white. Their portraits hung in the entrance hall, all stern and serious.

St. Peter's was a paying school, which meant Binti's father had to pay for school fees as well as for uniforms and books, but Binti and Junie would not have been allowed to go there if they had not been

good students. Kwasi went to St. Mark's, a private
school for boys.

St. Peter's was separated into the primary school,
which went to Standard Eight, and the secondary
school, which went to Form Four. "We are lucky you
are in St. Peter's," their father often said, "otherwise
we would have had to send Junie away to get her
secondary education." There were many days when
Binti would have liked that. Most secondary schools
in Malawi were boarding schools, because so few people could get in and they came from far away. But
having Junie go away to school meant Binti would
have to go away, too, eventually, and she wouldn't
want that. She liked things the way they were.

Binti liked being a student at St. Peter's. She liked
people seeing her in her uniform almost as much as
she liked them seeing her with her Story Time script.

Each morning at St. Peter's began with a school
assembly. There was always a hymn and a prayer at
the start, and the day ended with the singing of the
school song. In between there were other things, like
announcements. If one of the students turned in a
very good essay, or showed improvement in math,
they were brought up on the platform and everyone
applauded. Sometimes the choir sang a new song
they had been rehearsing, or a student who was learning how to play a musical instrument would play a
piece of music. Once a week, the prefect captains
would give a report on their school's conduct.

Today, the Anti-AIDS Club put on a play they had written about a girl who decides that having a boyfriend is more important than studying. The girl dropped out of school and ended up with AIDS. At the end of the play, the cast faced the audience and yelled in unison, "Virgin Power! Virgin Pride! Stop AIDS Now!" It was a good play, and got lots of applause. Binti applauded with enthusiasm. It helped to warm her up.

After the play, the Head Girl made the announcements about club meetings and other school business, then Binti got up to give the Junior Prefect's report.

"The Junior Prefect's Captain is ill with malaria. She asked me to deliver her report." Binti liked the way her voice sounded as it was projected through the hall. She hoped everyone noticed how well she spoke into the microphone. Maybe she'd be asked to deliver the report even when the Captain was well.

She read from the Captain's notes. "There has been too much noise in the junior school hallway lately. Teachers are complaining that students are talking in the hallways while classes are on. This must stop." Binti paused for a moment, to give her message something the Director would call a good effect. "Also, sweet wrappers have been found on the playground again. If this does not stop, we will not be allowed to bring sweets to school."

After a warning to stop running in the hall, Binti retook her seat.

"What was that pause?" the Head Girl asked her in a whisper. "Did you lose your place? Use your finger as a pointer next time. You looked lost up there."

Binti wished she could fall through the floor.

On her way through the hall after the assembly, she heard Glynnis, one of her classmates, say in a mocking tone of voice, "Oh, no, I dropped a sweet wrapper! I've committed a terrible crime!"

Binti spun around, against her better judgement, but all the girls behind her were smiling sweetly. Binti faced front again, and heard them laughing at her.

"She thinks she's so great because she's on the radio," Glynnis said. "I should go on the radio, too. I'd be better than *she* is."

This time, Binti pretended not to hear, but inside, she was panicking. That couldn't happen, could it? Someone so horrible, so ordinary, as Glynnis doing what Binti did? Binti felt sour and wormy all over, then she relaxed. Glynnis was not a good reader, and you had to be a good reader to be on a radio show. Glynnis would never go on.

Sometimes the show needed other children, but Binti was always careful not to let anyone in her school know. The radio show was hers, and she wasn't about to share.

Binti made a quick detour to the clothes box in the office, then hurried off to her classroom.

Chapter Four

"WHERE IS YOUR FATHER?"

Binti walked into the coffin yard after school that day to find angry customers standing there.

"I don't know," Binti said. "He can't be far. Can I help you?"

"We were here yesterday and ordered a coffin. We need that coffin now. The funeral is this afternoon."

Binti knew where her father kept his record books. "May I know your name, please?"

The man gave his name. "I paid in advance," he added.

Binti found the name, and also saw the checkmark in the column that showed her father had completed the coffin. "Your coffin is right over here," she said, leading them to a pile of several coffins stacked at the side of the yard. She checked the tags, found the right one, and stood aside while the men carried it away.

She watched them go, then went inside the little house to see if her father was there.

He was. He was on his bed, asleep.

Binti covered him with a blanket, and closed the door to his bedroom. Then she changed out of her school uniform and into her old skirt, shirt, and sweater. She put the kettle on, hoping her father would be awake by the time it boiled, and rinsed out her uniform blouse so that it would be fresh for school the next day. Mrs. Chintu could spot an unwashed blouse from all the way across the schoolyard.

Her father wasn't awake by the time the water had boiled, so she made tea for herself and took it out to the yard. She put it to one side to cool, and had just picked up the broom to tidy the yard when more customers arrived.

Binti gave out two more coffins, and collected two payments, before Kwasi came home from school.

"Where's Bambo?" he asked.

"He's asleep."

"In the middle of the day? Is he sick again?"

"He was asleep when I got home. I guess he's just tired."

Kwasi picked up the cup of tea Binti had set aside and took a swallow. "This is cold."

"It's also mine," Binti said. "I forgot about it."

Kwasi drank the rest of the tea anyway. He went inside to get changed out of his school uniform. Binti swept the yard. Although Junie wouldn't sit her senior class exams for many months yet, she stayed late for extra classes and review. But she would be home soon, and she could get Bambo out of bed.

Binti made more tea, and Kwasi went down the

road to buy boiled eggs and fried potatoes from the food stands for supper. By the time he returned, Junie was back.

After glaring at Binti and Kwasi for no good reason that Binti could see, Junie plopped her books on the table, and went in to see their father. "Make me some fresh tea," she said over her shoulder.

Kwasi lit the kerosene stove and set the kettle on it. Junie re-appeared. "Bambo's fever is up." She instructed Kwasi to sponge their father down with cool water, to try to lower his temperature. "We must make him drink a lot."

"What about medicine?" Binti asked.

"There is some left over from the last time he was sick," Junie said. She pulled out a chair and sat down, holding her head in her hands. When she raised herself back up again to bark out more orders, Binti saw the fear in her face, and didn't give her any arguments.

Binti and the others were quiet while they did their homework. The quiet was broken by their father coughing in the next room. Every now and then, one of them would go into the room to get their father to drink more tea.

"Bambo hasn't been sick for a long time," Binti said, unable to concentrate on her arithmetic assignment. "He hasn't been sick since Easter."

"He's been sick," Junie said. She had given up pretending to do the chemistry and was absent-mindedly sketching a wedding dress for herself. She'd been drawing wedding dresses for two years. This latest version had the high neckline and long sleeves Junie loved to wear, and some sort of billowing cape around it. "He just kept working."

"Well, then, he hasn't been sick like *this* since last Easter."

"How would you know?" Junie snapped. "You spend all your time thinking about that radio show. You think you're so important."

Kwasi slammed his English book shut and went outside. He hated being around when people were arguing. Binti watched him go, wishing she could hold her tongue the way he did.

But her tongue kept wagging in spite of her wishes. "And all *you* think about is your stupid wedding. It gets fancier and fancier every time you talk about it. No wonder our father is sick, working all the time to pay for your wedding."

"For your information, Miss Radio Star, I intend to get a job when I finish high school, and pay for the wedding myself. Both Noel and I will pay. It's the modern way of doing things, especially when the parents have a lot of worthless children who are burdens to them."

"Worthless? I'm earning money, and I'm only thirteen."

"When I was thirteen, I had already been looking after you and Kwasi—and the house—for three years."

The argument escalated to raised voices and hands slamming on the table. Binti lost track of what she was saying, and what the argument was even about.

The only thing that silenced them was the appearance of their father in the doorway.

"I have such a headache," he said quietly.

Binti paused mid-sentence. Her father looked like a gray ghost, all caved in on himself.

"I'll get you some tablets," Junie said.

Binti helped him back to bed. His skin was hot, but he was shivering badly. She fetched another blanket and spread it over him, then stood by the bed, not sure what to do next.

Junie told her. "Get out of the way," she said, coming into the bedroom with the headache tablets and a cup of water.

Binti got out of the way.

She went out into the yard. She knew Kwasi would be there. He was much easier to be around than Junie.

Kwasi was painting a coffin. His face still bore traces of worry, but it was starting to get dreamy, the way it always did when he did his art.

Most of the coffins their father sold were bare wood. "Our customers are not rich people," he said, "but they are good people who deserve the best we can give them." Even the bare wood coffins had been sanded until the wood was smooth and soft to the touch.

Whenever there was spare time from filling orders, their father made coffins for the stock room, in different sizes. Sometimes people didn't have time to place an order, and they needed a coffin right away. There were always extra coffins in the shed at Heaven Shop Coffins.

"We want people to know they can come to us at any time and we will have what they need. They will come back to us again, and they will tell other people, too."

Kwasi painted some of these stock coffins. For a little extra money, a customer could buy a coffin that had been painted plain blue or green. For more money, they could buy one with birds painted on it—Kwasi's specialty.

Binti couldn't draw, or do any fancy work, but she could paint. She got a brush, opened a can of blue, and lifted one of the little baby coffins to the table to work on.

"Wait," her brother said. He took a pen out of his pocket and drew a small bird in the bottom of the coffin. "Now you can paint it."

"Why do you always draw a bird in the bottom? I'm just going to paint over it."

"The bird will help the baby fly up to heaven faster," Kwasi told her.

Binti dipped her brush in the paint, and spread the color over the wood with slow, smooth strokes. She thought about the baby who would be put gently into the coffin, wrapped up against the cold of the grave. In her mind she saw birds lift the baby up and fly with it over the trees and into the blueness of the sky, bluer than the paint she was using.

Binti and her brother painted side by side. Now and then, the sound of their father's coughing mixed with the sound of their paintbrushes against the wood, and then it faded out again.

Chapter Five

"LADIES AND GENTLEMEN, I would now like to introduce to you the cast of 'Gogo's Family.'"

Binti stood with the rest of the cast just out of sight of the audience, and waited for Mr. Wajiru to call out her name. Her stomach was all fluttery.

The restaurant at the Meridian Mount Soche Hotel had been turned into a radio studio for the evening.

"This is a special occasion," Mr. Wajiru had told everyone at the planning meeting for tonight. "Story Time has been on the air for six months. It is a good reason for a party. We will all dress up. We are part of Malawi's culture. I want us to dress like Malawi."

Although she couldn't see him while he was talking on the stage, Binti knew the director was wearing his yellow, blue, and orange shirt. All the cast members wore African clothes. Binti wore a dress made out of chintje, the brightly-dyed Malawian cloth. Many of the people in the audience wore traditional dress, too. Binti thought they all looked like bright, happy flowers.

The audience was full of important people. "Some of these people are our funders," Mr. Wajiru said, "and some are people we want to fund us." There were even some foreign diplomats who had come from Malawi's capital, Lilongwe, for the event. Best of all, Binti's family was out there.

"Is that your father who was talking to you earlier?" Stewart whispered. He was standing beside her, waiting for his name to be called.

"Yes, it is," Binti whispered back. "Shhh."

"He's got the Slim," Stewart said. Slim was what many people called AIDS. "My uncle had it and he looked like that."

Binti thumped him on the chest. "Shut up, donkey!"

"Hey!" Stewart protested. He would have been heard by the audience if the amplified voice of Mr. Wajiru hadn't drowned him out.

The woman who played Gogo pulled Binti firmly by an arm. "Calm yourself," she said. "You're about to go on stage. Do you want the audience to see you like this?"

Binti didn't. She took some deep breaths like she'd been taught to do at Story Time.

The director first introduced the cast members who played small, irregular roles. Stewart was introduced with them. Then he introduced people who had bigger roles. Binti kept expecting her name to be called, but others went before her. Soon there was only her and the woman who played Gogo left.

"Playing young Kettie, here's Binti Phiri."

The applause suddenly got much louder. Binti ran up onto the stage. ("Move like you've got energy," the director said at the rehearsal.) She waved at the audience. She saw her family at one of the tables. They were applauding, too. Her father couldn't applaud that hard if he had AIDS, could he? Stewart was a donkey.

Of course, the loudest applause was reserved for Gogo herself. The woman who played the grandmother joined the rest of them on stage.

The cast stood in a line and held hands, then took a brief bow together. Then they took their places.

"We'll be recording onto tape, like in the studio," the director had told them, "so if you make a mistake, don't worry. We'll patch it together before we broadcast."

Binti was determined to not make any mistakes, not in front of all these people, and especially not in front of Stewart.

The opening music came up. The director had given the introductions in English, but the performance was, as always, in Chichewa, the language most Malawians spoke. It was a new thing for everybody, performing in front of so many people, away from the cozy privacy of the studio. Most of the other cast members made mistakes. They stumbled over a word, or lost their place in the script.

Binti hoped the people in the audience were

noticing that *she* never made an error. Maybe there was someone watching who could give her an even bigger job in radio some day, or perhaps even television.

She got so caught up in thinking about how famous she'd be that she missed her next cue. She stopped daydreaming, and paid attention, and didn't make any more mistakes.

———

"You remember my family, don't you, Mr. Wajiru?" At the dinner party that followed the taping, the director came over to Binti's table to say hello to everyone.

"Of course I do. Mr. Phiri," he shook Bambo's hand, "and Junie and Kwasi. Kwasi, that picture you painted for me gets more beautiful every day."

Kwasi, too shy to answer, smiled his lop-sided smile and looked down at his plate.

Mr. Wajiru pulled up a chair between Binti and her father. Next to healthy, lively Mr. Wajiru, Binti's father looked very, very thin. "I have a surprise for you," he said to Binti. He slid across a copy of the Youth Times. "The interview with you is in this month's edition. Page five. I hope you give Binti a lot of chores at home to keep her from getting a swelled head," he said to Bambo.

"Too late for that," Junie said. Binti frowned at her, but everyone else laughed.

"Don't worry," her father said. "I work them all very hard."

Binti opened the paper. There was a photo of her, standing by the microphone, pretending to read from the script. Binti thought she looked very professional and important, like a music star or a Prime Minister. "How many people read this?" she asked.

"You look fine," Bambo said. "We'll read the article later. The light is too dim in here to read it now."

"I have already read it," Mr. Wajiru said. "The writer did a good job. It is wonderful to see the exciting young journalists Malawi is growing these days."

The adults switched to talk of football, and Binti turned her attention to her food. Life at home was nice, but to live like *this* every day! How glorious that would be! Binti felt so good, she wanted to pass it on.

"That's your new dress, isn't it?" she asked Junie. "It looks wonderful on you." Binti had seen her sister piecing the dress together from parts of several ugly ones she had found at the secondhand stalls.

Junie flinched at the unusual compliment. Binti started eating again, but out of the corner of her eye, she saw Junie glance at her reflection in a wall mirror. Junie adjusted her collar and smiled.

Mr. Wajiru and her father moved from football to politics, and after a few moments of that, the director got up and shook hands again. "May I borrow Binti for a moment?" he asked Bambo.

"Certainly."

Binti followed the director to a spot along the side of the room. He bent down to speak with her.

"Binti, take your father home."

Binti didn't understand.

"He is very ill," the director said. "Take him home."

Binti didn't want to leave the party. She didn't want Stewart to be right. "He was sick, but he's better now. He says he's better."

"He is saying that so he doesn't spoil your evening. He has done a kind thing. Now you need to do a kind thing in return, and take him home. He will resist you, but you must tell him you want to. Can you act like you want to?"

There was no way to say no to Mr. Wajiru. "I'll take him home."

"I knew you would do the right thing," he said, and then Binti knew she had to be convincing.

"Bambo, I'm very tired. Can we go home?"

It took some persuading, but Binti was successful. Mr. Wajiru winked at her as he saw them into a taxi. Her father seemed to shrink even more on the ride home. Kwasi and Junie both had to support him on the walk from the car to the house. He went right to bed.

Binti and her brother and sister changed out of their good clothes. Binti made tea, and they sat together at the kitchen table.

"You and your stupid anniversary," Junie said.

"You completely wore him out by making him go."

"Shut up," Kwasi said. "There was no way he was not going. This isn't Binti's fault."

"You two always stick together." Junie took her tea into the little room she shared with Binti. Kwasi took his to the couch where he slept. Binti sat alone at the table.

She took out the copy of the Youth Times, and turned it to the article and photo of herself. She touched the photo of her face with her finger. The quiet of the house settled around her, broken only by the sound of her father's labored breathing.

Chapter Six

BINTI'S FATHER DID NOT FEEL BETTER THE NEXT DAY, or the next. When the children went alone to church, and told people in the congregation that their father was ill, some of the church ladies brought over food and looked in on him. Their pastor came and sat with him one evening. But a lot of people in the congregation were sick. The pastor and the church ladies even had people in their own families who were very ill. They could not fix things for the children.

They took turns staying home from school to look after Bambo and to look after the shop. The collection of coffins in the storeroom dwindled. Kwasi tried making more, but all he did was waste lumber. Binti managed to put together a baby coffin, but it was lop-sided, and the joints were not tight enough. It fell apart when she carried it from the worktable to the shed. A task her father had done with such ease was still too difficult for them.

New customers came, and went away empty-handed. They were not very upset. There were a lot of coffin makers in Blantyre they could choose from.

Binti resented Mr. Tsaka. She imagined him getting rich off her father's customers.

In the end, though, it was Mr. Tsaka who came to their aid.

"My customers tell me your father is ill," he told Binti, who was taking her turn at staying home. "May I see him?"

Binti was too tired to argue. She led the way to her father's bedroom.

Mr. Tsaka greeted her father respectfully, as though Bambo was standing at his worktable as usual. Her father replied as best he could, but he was very weak.

"Can't you see how sick he is?" Mr. Tsaka asked Binti when he came back out into the yard. "Why isn't he in the hospital?"

He softened his tone when he saw the alarm in Binti's face.

"Does your family have money to pay for a private hospital?"

She shook her head. "It's all gone to the cousins."

"I wish I had the money to pay for your father to go to one," Mr. Tsaka said. "I like your father. He is a good man and an honest businessman. But my money is all tied up in coffins for my business. He'll have to go to the public hospital."

"I don't know how to do that." Binti could feel herself starting to cry.

"I will take you. Gather up blankets and things your father will need. Bring some for yourself. Leave a note for your brother and sister. I will be right back."

Binti did as Mr. Tsaka suggested. Gathering blankets was easy, but what else would her father need? There were some headache tablets left, and she got them.

"Take some clean clothes for him," Mr. Tsaka said when he returned. He bent down to talk to her father. He spoke quietly and gently. He held Bambo in a sitting position so Binti could wrap blankets around his shoulders.

"Did you gather some things for yourself?" he asked.

"I don't know what you mean."

"You will have to stay at the hospital and take care of your father. There are not enough nurses. Take a blanket for yourself, and anything else you think you would need. Take your school books, too. Your father would not want you falling behind in your studies."

Binti took the blanket from her bed, and rolled it up to make it easier to carry. She fetched her book bag, and added this week's "Gogo's Family" script. She couldn't think what else to take.

He told Binti to put blankets down in the back of his pickup truck. "Get in first so you can support your father's head," he told her. Bambo was all bones in a blanket. Mr. Tsaka carried him tenderly, the way the little boy had carried his puppy.

Binti climbed into the truck, and sat with her back against the side. Mr. Tsaka lifted Bambo up, and put him gently down on the blankets. Binti rested his head in her lap, and tightened the blankets around him.

Mr. Tsaka got into the front of the truck and began to drive. In some places, the road was bumpy. Binti tried to keep her father comfortable.

The hospital was on the other side of Blantyre. The trip took a long time. They drove by the Story Time house. Binti strained her neck to look, but no one was outside to see her pass by.

Mr. Tsaka had to park the truck around the back of the hospital.

"Hurry!" Binti urged him on as he carried her father into the main entrance. There was a line of people in the hallway, sitting on the floor.

"You'll have to go to the back of the line," a man said, holding up a woman with closed eyes. "We have been waiting a long time."

"But this is my father. He's sick," Binti protested.

"This is my wife. *She* is sick." The man waved a fly away from his wife's face.

They went to the back of the line. Mr. Tsaka put Bambo gently on the floor, his head again in Binti's lap.

"I can't stay here with you," he said. "I have customers coming and no way to tell them to come back another time."

Binti understood about customers, but she didn't like watching him leave.

"There are not enough nurses," the woman beside Binti said. She had a baby slung in front of her in a *chintje*. A younger woman sitting beside her kept slumping over.

There was not a lot of talking. More sick people came in, and there started to be a line on the other side of Binti, too. Sometimes healthy people would walk in, fast, erect, important. Once, three people walked slowly out, leaning on each other. Binti heard crying in the parking lot.

"My daughter is HIV-positive," the woman next to Binti said. "It's in her blood. I want the doctors to take out her bad blood and give her new blood."

Binti looked more closely at the woman's daughter. Bambo didn't look anything like as bad as she did. Stewart didn't know anything.

A nurse finally came. She walked down the line, taking names of patients, and looking at how ill they were. When she got to Binti's father, she made a decision quickly.

"Can I have help to carry this man into the examining room?" Two men from the line stood up. Binti could see they were ill, but not as ill as her father. They picked her father up off the floor, and followed the nurse. Binti picked up their things, and followed her father.

Her father was placed on one of the cots. Binti stood by and held his hand. The doctor finished examining the other patients in the room, and finally got to Binti's father.

"He's very sick," the doctor said. She put her

hand on Binti's shoulder. "Why don't you wait in the hall while I take a look at him?"

"He doesn't have AIDS, though," Binti stated. "It's something else. Someone said he has AIDS, but I'm sure he doesn't, so you don't have to check him for that."

"You're sure he doesn't have AIDS?" the doctor replied, washing her hands. "Eighty percent of the people who come into this hospital have AIDS—but you're sure your father is the exception?" She put a blood pressure belt around Bambo's thin arm. "Thirty percent of the people in our cities are HIV-positive, almost half of Malawi's civil servants are HIV-positive, and our health care workers and our teachers are dying of AIDS faster than they can be replaced."

The doctor looked at Binti's face, sighed, and stopped her tirade.

"We will test your father's blood for the AIDS virus," the doctor said, but this time she spoke gently. "We do that with everybody who comes in. If he has it, we cannot cure him of it, but we can give him drugs that will make him feel better. Please wait out in the hall. It will be all right."

Binti didn't know how the doctor could say it would be all right. She stood out in the hallway with her back against the wall. She knew the other sick people waiting in line were looking at her, probably hoping the doctor would hurry and finish with her father so that they could be treated. Binti didn't look at them. She looked down at her shoes.

"You can come back in," the doctor said. She handed Binti a bottle of pills. "Your father has pneumonia. You need to give him one of these pills every six hours. Do you have any older people coming to be with you here?"

"My brother and sister will come."

"Tell them what I am telling you. If you need help, there will be women in the ward caring for their own family members. Get them to help you. There are not enough nurses."

"So Bambo doesn't have AIDS?" Binti thought that was what she was hearing. "He will get better?"

"We'll know soon if he's strong enough to fight the pneumonia. We have no drugs to fight the AIDS, if he has it. We test everyone for our own information. These pills are the best thing we can give him right now." Two men, not the sick men but hospital orderlies, carried her father out of the examining room on a stretcher. "Follow these men," the doctor said. "They will find a space for your father."

The public hospital was a series of one-story buildings linked together by long hallways, like spokes on a crazy wheel. They went to several wards until they found one with room for her father.

"He can stay here," a nurse in a white uniform said, on her way to another ward.

Binti looked around. The ward had four sections divided by low walls, each packed with beds that faced each other. There was almost no space between beds, and every bed was full.

She turned to ask the nurse just where her father was supposed to go, but she had already gone.

"Come over here. There is room here."

An old woman in a *chintje* skirt took Binti by the arm to the far section of the room. She pointed to a space on the floor between two of the beds. Someone put a green rubber mat over the concrete. The two men put down the stretcher and gently lifted her father onto the mat.

"He needs a pillow," the woman said. "I have an extra." She fetched her spare pillow and made Binti's father more comfortable. "This is your father?"

Binti nodded.

"You are alone in the world with him?"

"I have an older brother and sister," Binti said, then she panicked "I forgot to leave them a note! They will come home from school and find us gone, and they won't know where we are!"

"Calm down," the woman said. "Keep your voice low so that people can rest. We all have reason to yell and scream. Your father has probably been ill for a long time. You have no money for a private hospital, or you wouldn't be here. They will know where to look, and they will find you. You look after your father. They will come to you. Come, I will show you where to find the things you need. My name is Mrs. Nyika."

"My name is Binti."

Mrs. Nyika showed Binti where the water taps

were in the ward, and where the toilet was, in the hall just outside the ward. The toilet smelled very bad.

"You can wash his things out and spread them in the sun to dry, when you have to." She pointed to the window. In the yard outside the ward, Binti saw blankets, sheets, and articles of clothing spread on the sparse grass and over bushes. There were people in the yard, too, sitting up or lying down. The sun was shining, but they were bundled up against the chiperoni. "On warmer days, you father might like to be out in the sunshine. What is his work?"

"He makes coffins."

"So he is used to being out in the open air."

They went back to her father's bed. "Who are you here with?" Binti asked.

"I'm here with my son," Mrs. Nyika told her. "This is him, this is my John." John was in a real bed, across the aisle from Binti's father. Binti thought he was a few years older than Junie, but not many. It was hard to tell because he was so thin. She shook his hand. It was like shaking hands with a weed.

"I have a niece in another ward," Mrs. Nyika said. "She has just finished nurse's school, but she is dying. All the young people around me are dying. God's plan is a mystery, but we must have faith that He knows what He is doing."

Binti had gone to church every Sunday of her life. One thing she was certain of—God did not want her father to die. He wanted her father to get better and get back to work so that he'd be in the coffin yard when Binti got home from school, sanding down a board and greeting her with, "How's my famous daughter today?"

She left Mrs. Nyika fussing with her son's blankets, and fussed with her father's. "We won't be here long," she told him. "They'll make you better, and we'll go home again."

Her father opened his eyes. "Don't be afraid," he said. "You are a good daughter, and you are doing everything right." He closed his eyes again. Talking had worn him out.

Binti sat on the mattress beside her father. There was no place else to sit. From their spot on the floor, she could see people's feet as they walked by.

She looked beside her, to the man lying on the mat between the next two beds. An older woman was sitting with him. The older woman looked back at her, with nothing in her face but tiredness.

"When can my father have a real bed?" Binti asked her.

"When someone gets better, or when someone dies," the woman answered, then looked away again.

Binti could see the number of patients sleeping on the floor. She counted the number of people in proper beds. Unless a lot of people got well or died soon, her father would be stuck on the floor for a long time.

Binti got some water and gave her father one of the pills.

"You'll want to give him more pills than the doctor told you to," Mrs. Nyika said, "but they don't work that way. Give him just what you were told to give him."

Binti promised she would. She stayed close to her father, dozing beside him on and off for the rest of the afternoon as she waited for the pill to do its job.

"You're crowding him!" a sharp voice said.

Binti was startled out of her sleep. Junie was standing at the foot of her father's mat, her hands on her hips. Kwasi was beside her, but he didn't look angry, just sad.

Binti got to her feet. She tripped a little on the edge of the mat on her way out to the aisle. Junie took Binti's place beside her father. Her voice had woken him up, too. He spoke quietly with Junie.

"Are you all right?" Kwasi asked.

Binti nodded. "How did you know we were here?" she asked, but she didn't need him to answer. She saw Mr. Tsaka on the other side of the room, talking with one of the other patients.

Junie stood up, and motioned for Kwasi to talk to their father. "What did the doctor say?" Junie asked Binti.

"Bambo has pneumonia," Binti said. "They tested his blood for AIDS, but they don't know yet if he has that. I don't know if they'll tell us if he has it."

"What are they doing for him? Did they give him any medicine?"

Binti took the bottle of pills out of her sweater

pocket. "He's supposed to have one of these every six hours."

"And when did he have the last one?"

Binti started to cry. "I don't know! I don't know what time it is!"

Junie shook her head, took the pills from her and went to get some water.

"Binti, come here," her father said. She sat beside Kwasi. "Tomorrow you tape your show. I want you to go home with Junie tonight and get a good sleep. Come back tomorrow after the show, and tell me all about it."

"I don't want to leave you."

"Kwasi will stay with me tonight," he said. "I will still be here tomorrow. Do as I say. Let me talk to your sister now."

Junie had his pill ready. Binti watched Kwasi hold him up so he could swallow it easily.

They stayed for a little while longer, then said good night. "I'll see you tomorrow, my famous daughter," he said. "Bring your script back with you and read it to me."

Binti looked back as she, Junie, and Mr. Tsaka left the ward, but since her father was on the floor, she couldn't see him.

———

Mr. Wajiru was not surprised to hear that her father

was in the hospital. "He told you to come to the taping today, so he wants you to do well. Don't disappoint him. Put your worry away in a pocket, and do the best job you can do."

As the first rehearsal began, Mr. Wajiru spoke to the cast. "Binti's father is in the hospital, and she is very worried about him. We are glad she came here today. All of us have things in our lives that are difficult and we all have days when we don't think we can do what is asked of us. There is an old saying in show business: The show must go on. Binti has shown us today exactly what that means. Now, let us begin."

After that, Binti felt a little calmer. Although her worry didn't disappear, she was able to put it away for a while, and have a good show.

Junie had spent the day with Kwasi at the hospital, taking a minibus there early in the morning. They both looked tired when Binti got there with Mr. Tsaka.

"Where did you sleep?" Binti asked her brother.

"Under the bed, beside Bambo. It was uncomfortable, but I was happier to be here with him than at home, worrying. I did a drawing of him while he was sleeping." He took a piece of paper out of his pants pocket and unfolded it.

Binti looked at it. "He looks like he's smiling."

"He's seeing Mama," Kwasi said.

"Kwasi, take Junie outside for some sunshine," their father said. "Binti and I will visit for a while."

"We'll be back soon," Junie said, on their way out.

Binti sat beside their father. "The pills are working," she said. "You seem better today."

"I am better," he said. "Do you know what would make me feel better still? To hear you read the script from today's show."

Binti got her script. She began to read.

"Read it louder," Mrs. Nyika said. "Your father has been bragging about you. Let us all hear it."

Binti read a little louder.

"Here. Stand on this." Someone fetched a chair and put it in the middle of the aisle.

Binti felt a little foolish, but her father nodded at her, so she stepped onto the chair.

"In a nice, loud voice, now," Mrs. Nyika said.

Binti took a deep breath. "This week's story is called 'Gogo Settles an Argument.'"

Binti read in a loud voice. She read all the parts. The ward was silent as the patients and the family members who cared for them listened to her. Sometimes the silence was broken by laughter. When she got to the end, people clapped. Binti bowed, like she did that night at the hotel, and stepped down from the chair.

"That was wonderful," her father said. "You will do great things with your life." He closed his eyes.

Binti leaned against him. It felt good to be close.

Junie and Kwasi came back in. They sat at the side of the mat wherever they could find space. They didn't talk. They just sat with their father while he slept.

Two orderlies brought in a cart of food. Junie got a bowl out of her bag and handed it to Binti. "Line up," she said. Binti joined the line and got some nsima and beans. Junie woke their father up, but he didn't want to eat, and went back to sleep right away. Binti and her brother and sister shared the bowl of food. Junie had brought forks with her, too.

Later that evening, a preacher came into the ward. He smiled broadly as he went from bed to bed. He held his Bible in one hand, and reached out to comfort with the other. He preached about the gift of joy, and the love of God. "Praise God and love Him. Love each other. Do good in the world." He started to sing, a song of prayer and praise, clapping a hand against his Bible to keep time.

The patients and their families joined in. Some danced as they sang. Mrs. Nyika held out her hands for Binti, Junie, and Kwasi to dance with her. As she danced, Binti could see that even patients who were too weak to clap were singing the prayer along with everybody else. Many people were smiling. Some were crying. Binti was doing both. Music rose in the ward as the patients, visitors, and preacher thanked God for all that is good.

Some time during the song Binti's father passed away.

"He died on the floor, but he was surrounded by music and by people who loved him," said the pastor, as he knelt with them to pray. "Many are the kings whose death was not as good."

Chapter Seven

RELATIVES DESCENDED ON THE HOUSE. Uncles and aunts and adult cousins from Lilongwe, Monkey Bay, and even Kasungu started flooding into the coffin yard. Junie kept Binti busy fetching and cleaning.

"Where will they all sleep?" she worried.

"They can all sleep in the road," Binti declared. "I don't know them, and I don't want them here. How did they get here, anyway?"

"Kwasi called them from the hospital, and I don't care what you want or don't want. There's a right way to do things, and that's what we're going to do."

"It's *our* father who's dead," Binti grumbled. She was helping Junie to prepare the midday meal. "*They* should be doing things for *us!*"

"I did this all by myself when Mama died, and I was younger then than you are now," Junie said. "Don't complain to me."

Kwasi came into the little kitchen area carrying a stack of books.

"They keep taking our things," he said. "They

keep picking up our things and putting them in their bags." He took the books into the bedroom and came out again.

"They're strangers and they *steal*," Binti said. Why wasn't Junie chasing them away?

"I remember some of them from Mama's funeral," Kwasi said. "Don't you?"

"I only remember the crowd," Binti said. "I remember how the house felt when they were here, and how empty it felt when they left. It felt like they swooped down on our house and took Mama away with them."

Junie shoved past them to get to a bowl. "Could you two at least work while you talk?"

Binti shoved her back. "Work, work, work. Don't you care that our father is dead?"

Junie slapped her right across the face and left the kitchen.

Kwasi left, too. Binti chopped up a tomato, then put down the knife. A tear fell on the tomato. "Why should I cook for all these people?" she asked herself. She left the meal unprepared and went out into the coffin yard.

"What are you doing?" she asked Kwasi, who was carrying a piece of lumber to the worktable. He was ignoring the relatives that were sitting around the yard, waiting to be fed.

"I'm building Bambo a coffin," he said. "He needs one, and I'm going to build him one."

"But you're no good at it," Binti reminded him. "Neither am I."

"I just wasn't trying very hard before," Kwasi said. "If I try harder, I can build one, a good one. So that's what I'm going to do."

There was no talking him out of it. In his own way, Kwasi was as stubborn as Junie.

"What are you doing, son?" One of the uncles—Binti still hadn't gotten them sorted out in her mind, having just met them—put his hand on Kwasi's arm, just as Kwasi was about to start sawing a board.

"I'm building my father a coffin."

"I don't think we want any of those boards sawed up," the uncle said. "They are worth money, and I don't think you know what you are doing."

"I do," Kwasi protested.

"You are a schoolboy, not a working boy." The uncle took the saw out of Kwasi's hand.

Binti hated to see the frustrated and defeated look on Kwasi's face. "Come on," she said. "I have an idea."

She got her radio money out of the cup on the top shelf in the kitchen. The women in the house watched her do it.

"What money is that? Where are you going with it? When are you going to finish cooking dinner?"

Binti ignored their questions and pulled away from their reaching hands. She took her brother's arm and walked quickly out of the yard.

They went to Mr. Tsaka's coffin yard.

"I can guess why you're here," Mr. Tsaka said. "I am sad that your father cannot be buried in one of his own coffins. I know how he felt about my coffins. No, don't disagree!" he laughed. "Your father had many strong opinions. I enjoyed disagreeing with him. I wish I could give you a coffin for free, but I can't. I will, however, sell you one for what it cost me." He showed them some of the coffins he had put together.

"We want to put it together ourselves," Binti said.

Mr. Tsaka nodded. "Yes, you must do that. Come and choose your pieces, and I will show you what to do."

They chose a green one with delicate strokes of white in it. "It's made to look like marble," Mr. Tsaka said. "Marble is a very beautiful stone." He showed the children how to put the pieces together, and let them use his tools.

When it was done, Mr. Tsaka gave Kwasi a small brush and a tin of paint. "Your father told me what you do," he said.

Kwasi took the brush. He painted a beautiful bird in the bottom of the coffin. Its wings were spread, like it was flying high.

"Now, carry this back and show off to your relatives what you are capable of." Mr. Tsaka took some of Binti's money to pay for the coffin, and handed the rest back to her. "Keep this safe, and keep it hidden," he told her. "You never know when you may need it."

Kwasi and Binti picked up the coffin.

"I'll be by this afternoon to drive the ladies to the mortuary and then to the funeral," Mr. Tsaka said. Binti and Kwasi thanked him, and headed back to their own yard.

The relatives were impressed with the coffin, but— "You spent too much money!"

"The deal is done," Kwasi said. "This is for our father."

"Do you have any of that money left?" one of the aunts asked.

"There is no more money," Kwasi answered for Binti. "We had just enough for the coffin. Our neighbor will be here this afternoon to take us to the mortuary and to the funeral."

"You should put more respect in your voice when you talk to us," one of the uncles said. "You are just a boy, and you are missing your father, and you don't know us, but you should still have more respect in your voice."

Binti looked at her brother's face. He did look sad, but he no longer looked defeated.

"What is this bird painted here?" a relative asked.

Binti went inside to finish preparing the meal. Some of the aunts had already done it. They looked at her and shook their heads. Binti pretended not to notice, and got bowls out so the meal could be served.

"Wear your best dress," Junie said after dinner.

"It's not Sunday, but we will be in church." She had laid Binti's clothes out for her.

Binti changed, and when she was ready, she joined Junie and the other women. Everyone was dressed up. Mr. Tsaka came. Binti and the others climbed into the back of the pickup truck. The men lifted the coffin across their laps. There wasn't room for all of the women to sit. Some stood up, hanging onto the truck however they could. Kwasi and two of the boy cousins near his age hopped up and perched on the very back edge of the truck.

Binti sat beside Junie, the coffin sitting across their legs. Binti held onto it tightly, although with so many women holding it, it could not possibly fall off the truck.

The women started singing, and kept on singing, all the way to the mortuary at the back of the hospital.

The men got out of the front of the truck, and Kwasi and the other boys hopped out of the back. They took the coffin inside. The women kept singing.

The coffin was heavier on Binti's lap when the truck left the mortuary. She thought of her father inside it. She wanted him to get up and out of the coffin so they could go home and make all the relatives leave. That didn't happen, so she joined in the singing and tried to keep from crying.

They had to wait outside when they got to the church. Another funeral was still finishing up. The other relatives joined them in the churchyard. Mr.

Wajiru found Binti there, and hugged her, and hugged Junie and Kwasi as well.

Finally, the service got underway. There were a lot of people in the church. A lot of people had liked Binti's father.

Binti, Kwasi, and Junie sat up in the front of the church. Their father's brothers and sisters sat with them. Binti could see that they were crying. It made her feel a little better about them. She tried not to think about her father being closed up in the coffin at the front of the church.

Binti, sitting near the aisle, looked back to see an old woman, walking slowly, supported by a young man.

Junie and Kwasi, along with the relatives and the rest of the congregation, stood up respectfully. Junie pulled Binti to her feet.

"Who's that?" Binti asked.

"You don't remember? That's Gogo."

Two of the uncles tried to steer Gogo into a seat with the family, but she shook them off. She and her companion kept walking right up to the front where the coffin was. The pastor spread his arms to embrace her, but she ignored him.

"Open it up," she directed the young man with her.

Two of Binti's uncles were at her side in a flash. She shook them away. "I want to see my boy," she insisted. "Help me to see my boy or leave me alone."

They helped the young man lift the coffin lid.

"That's him," Gogo said. "That's my son."

She turned to the congregation. "My young friend Jeremiah and I have just come from the hospital. The doctor told me there was AIDS in my boy's blood. He is the second son I have lost to AIDS. I have lost three daughters, too. All to the same thing. All to this AIDS."

Binti thought Gogo was going to cry, but the old woman swallowed her tears and kept on talking.

"We do not want to say what it is. We think that if we don't say it, it will go away, but it won't go away. In the old days, when there were still lions around, if a lion came into our village and carried away our young, we did not keep silent! If we were silent, it would keep eating our children. We had to make noise. We had to bang pots and yell, 'There is a lion in the village!' Then we could get rid of the lion and save our children.

"There is a lion in our village now. It is called AIDS. It is carrying away our children. So I want to say today, in front of all of you, that my son died of AIDS, and I loved him. His wife probably died of AIDS before him, and I loved her, too. And I am tired of burying my children."

"Amen!" the pastor said. He started praying, and people started singing. Gogo embraced Binti, Kwasi, and Junie, all of them together. Binti could feel her brother and sister crying. She cried, too.

There was a procession to the cemetery from the church. Binti danced with the others in the procession, while Kwasi helped to carry the coffin. The cemetery was shady and green. While her father was being lowered into the ground, Binti saw a large bird, its wings spread, soaring high into the sky.

Chapter Eight

"I SUPPOSE I CAN TAKE THE BOY."

Binti, lying in bed beside Junie, had just been drifting off to sleep when she heard one of the uncles speak. "He can work in my fishing business in Monkey Bay."

"Do you have room for him?"

"None of us has room for any of them," the uncle said, "but what can we do? They are our brother's children, and our mother expects us to look after them. She could not have been more clear about that."

Binti sat up. She shook Junie awake. "Listen," she whispered. "They're planning something." She woke up Kwasi, too, who was sleeping on a mat on the floor. He joined his sisters on the bed, and they listened.

"The boy doesn't seem like much of a worker," one of the aunts said. "I kept seeing him sitting by himself, wasting paper with those drawings of his. I don't think he'll be of much use to you."

"No, he probably won't be, but I have enough girls in my house already."

"I don't want any of them in my house," another aunt said. "How do we know *they* don't have AIDS? I don't want them infecting my children. We could drink out of the same cup, and all get sick."

"We have to do something. I have agreed to take the boy. Who will take the girls?"

Binti had heard enough. She jumped out of bed and into the front room.

"No one is taking any of us anywhere," Binti said. "We're staying here. We can look after ourselves."

"I don't like the temper on that one," an aunt said, squishing her face like Binti had a bad smell.

"Binti, come." Junie pulled her back into the bedroom and shut the door.

"Why did you do that?" Binti demanded.

"Will you stop acting like such a child?"

"Will the two of you stop arguing?" Kwasi pushed himself between them. "Do we have any choices here?" he asked Junie.

Junie paced around the room before finally sitting on the bed. Binti and Kwasi joined her there. "There's no money," Junie said. "There never was very much, and even though Binti paid for the coffin, there were funeral expenses and medical expenses."

"But I'll still be earning money," Binti reminded them.

"What about school?" Kwasi asked. "Are our fees paid up?"

"Our fees are paid until the end of next month," Junie told them. "If we can come up with a plan to take care of ourselves, maybe the uncles and aunts will let us stay together. I know it doesn't sound like it, but they're only trying to do what's right. We are a burden that they are trying to take care of properly. If we can prove we don't need them, I think they'll be very happy. After all, we own this house. We can't run the coffin business, but maybe we can rent it out to someone else who would like to run it."

"We could rent out Bambo's room, too," Binti suggested, then felt ashamed to have thought of someone else sleeping in her father's room.

Junie caught the look on Binti's face. "Bambo would want us to stay together. We'll find someone good to rent the room to—a teacher, perhaps, or maybe our pastor knows someone."

"Binti and I can switch to a free school," Kwasi offered. Binti hated the idea of changing schools, but not nearly as much as she hated the idea of being shipped off to one of the uncles or aunts. Besides, at a new school, she'd still enjoy special status as the girl on "Gogo's Family."

Kwasi turned to Binti. "But I think Junie should stay at St. Peter's until her exams are over. She'll earn more later if she graduates from a good school. I'll get a job in the market. We'll get by."

"We'll get by a whole lot better than a lot of people in Malawi," Junie said. "So, we have a plan. We'll manage this way until I write my exams. Maybe I can do some secretarial work at the school to reduce my fees, or make some arrangement to pay when I start working. After Noel and I are married, you two will live with us until you finish school. We thought you would probably have to do that, anyway, with Bambo being so ill."

"Did he have AIDS?" Binti asked.

"He had pneumonia," Junie said, firmly. "You heard what the doctor said."

"But Gogo said ..."

"Gogo is an old woman, and she was upset. Maybe she heard something at the hospital, maybe she didn't. If people ask, you tell them our father died of pneumonia."

"And Mama?"

"You tell them Mama died of TB. That's what I remember, and I was older than both of you when she died, so I remember best." Junie looked from Kwasi to Binti, to make sure they really heard her. "Well, let's go present our plan to the relatives. Once this is settled, we can all get some sleep, and tomorrow they can go on their way."

The children went out into the front room. The relatives filled what Binti used to think was a big room, where the family cooked, ate, and relaxed. The aunts and uncles who couldn't fit around the table spilled over to the sofa and chair—the chair that Bambo liked to sit in.

The children bowed respectfully, the girls bending one knee behind the other. Junie outlined their plan. She finished up by saying, "We're grateful for your concern, but you don't need to worry about us."

Uncle Mloza was the first to speak. He's the one Binti thought looked most like Bambo but taller and not as handsome. He was also the one sitting in Bambo's chair. "Your plan is good," he said, "but you're mistaken about many things. For one thing, you do not own this house—we do. We are the responsible adults, and your father's property comes to us."

"After all, he was our brother," said the aunt who didn't like Binti's temper.

"The house and the business are being sold. This is a good location, and we have already found a buyer."

"But the money from the house …" Junie began.

"Will come to us," Uncle Wysom finished. "We are responsible for your care."

Uncle Mloza went on. "We have obtained a refund from your schools. Our own children don't go to such fancy schools, so why should you? Kwasi will come with me to Monkey Bay. You girls will go together with your Uncle Wysom. He lives in Lilongwe. You will help with the household chores and make yourselves useful."

"What about my radio show?" Binti demanded. "I have to be on the radio."

"Yes, it's too bad about that. That is money we will have to say goodbye to." Uncle Wysom shifted around on the sofa to get more comfortable. "You tape the show on Saturdays, yes? I'll let you record one more show, then they will have to get somebody else. I have my own business and my own family to attend to. I cannot stay in Blantyre any longer than that."

Binti couldn't believe what she was hearing. Before she could say any words to express herself, she felt Junie's hand on her shoulder.

"We are grateful for your kind plan," Junie said, "but we still would prefer to stay together. My fiancé, Noel, would certainly agree to marry me sooner than we had planned if I ask him to. Kwasi and Binti will live with us. We'll manage."

"Ah, yes, Noel." Uncle Mzola took an open envelope out of his pocket. "Noel's brother delivered this to you earlier." He handed it to Junie.

"You have read it? It is addressed to me."

"What concerns you concerns us."

Junie read the note. She wilted so suddenly it was as though someone had hit her. She turned and went back into the bedroom.

Binti and Kwasi turned to follow her.

"Kwasi," Uncle Mzola said, "be up early in the morning. We will go to Monkey Bay tomorrow."

Binti and Kwasi shut the bedroom door behind

them. Junie was face down on the bed, sobbing. For a long while, Binti and Kwasi were too stunned to do anything. Then Binti leaned over and took the scrunched-up note out of Junie's hand.

She read it out loud. "Dear Junie: I am writing to break off our engagement. My parents do not want me to marry into a family that has been tainted with AIDS, and I must respect their wishes. Noel."

There was nothing to say.

Binti and Kwasi lay down beside their older sister, and Junie didn't push them away. They kept close together, all alone, and waited for the morning.

———

Uncle Mzola was eager to get going soon after the sun came up. He handed Junie his address. "I know you think we are being cruel, but we are doing the best we can. We loved your father and your mother." He nodded at the piece of paper in Junie's hand. "Stay in touch with your brother. Come and see us sometime."

"You don't have to go," Binti said to Kwasi.

"What choice do I have? There's nowhere else for me to be."

"Junie, do something!"

"None of us has any choices now," was all Junie would say. Her cardigan was buttoned wrong, but she didn't seem to notice.

They helped him pack. Binti made sure he had his pencils and his paint set. "There will be new things for you to paint in Monkey Bay," she said, "new birds, maybe."

He tucked them into his bag.

Binti had another thought. She checked to make sure none of the uncles or aunts were watching, then took the rest of her money out from where she had hidden it. She divided it into three. "Keep this hidden," she told Junie and Kwasi, handing them their shares. "It's us against them now."

"Let's go, son," Uncle Mloza called.

"I'm not your son," Kwasi muttered. He hugged Binti and Junie, took a last look around the house and the coffin yard, then followed Uncle Mloza down the road. Binti and Junie watched as he climbed into the minibus behind Uncle Mloza. He had time to wave once before the bus pulled away.

———

"Keep the pin," Headmistress Chintu said, closing Binti's fingers around her prefect pin. Binti and Junie had gone to St. Peter's School the next day to collect their things and say goodbye. "Keep it as something to remember us by."

To Junie, Mrs. Chintu said, "You are so close to getting your Secondary School Certificate. I hope you are able to write your exams, but even if you are not, remember that you have more education now than most people in Malawi. I trust you will use it well."

"Yes, Mrs. Chintu," Junie replied, in a voice that was flat and empty.

From the school, they went to the Story Time house.

"Mr. Wajiru will fix things," Binti said. "People like hearing me on the radio. I get letters. He can't let me go."

Mr. Wajiru listened to them quietly. "This is very sad news you are bringing me," he said.

"The uncles and aunts have cleared out most of our belongings," Binti said. "Kwasi kept taking them back and hiding them, but they got everything anyway. They've sold our father's house and business, and they're keeping the money for themselves."

Mr. Wajiru nodded that he understood. "Property grabbing happens too much in Malawi," he said. "Sometimes it is done out of greed, but sometimes it is done because there are great needs. We should do a show about it some time," he added, more to himself.

Binti jumped on that. "I could help with that show," she said. "I could live here with Junie. She's very good at cleaning and taking care of clothes, and I could … well, I could sweep and do the show. You wouldn't need to keep paying me. You could use my pay for rent. We wouldn't take up much room." She nudged Junie to get her to say something to help persuade him, but Junie kept silent and looked at the floor.

Mr. Wajiru pressed his fingers together while he thought. The longer he thought, the more hopeful Binti became. But she was disappointed.

"I wish I could offer you a place to live here," he said, "but that is not possible. I can't go against the wishes of your relatives. You are their family, and it's up to them to decide. Even if that were not the case, there is no place here where you can live."

Binti lost all hope.

"Here is what I can do," Mr. Wajiru offered. "We have three more scripts written and ready to record, in addition to tomorrow's show. Can you stay for a bit today? We can record your part, and splice it in later. That way, you will be paid for the shows, and you will be able to be part of 'Gogo's Family' a little while longer."

"I can do that," Binti said. She didn't want to ask if Mr. Wajiru would find another granddaughter for Gogo. She didn't want to know.

It was arranged that the director would drive Binti home after the tapings were done, so Junie went back to their house to pack. It was strange to be in the studio all by herself, with just Mr. Wajiru feeding her her cues. She wasn't as good as she would have been with a week of preparation and the whole cast around her, but Mr. Wajiru seemed satisfied. When he paid her, he said, "Keep the money safe and hidden."

He must have told the other cast members about Binti's leaving, because there was a farewell party after the next day's taping. Everyone had gifts for her, even Stewart, who maybe wasn't as awful as she thought before. She received books and pens, a new blouse, and tins of sweets. The show gave her a pair of new Chiperoni blankets, made by the company with the same name as the wind, one for her and one for Junie.

Uncle Wysom showed up at the radio house at the end of the day, just as Binti was being paid for that day's show. "That money will come to me," he said. "I am her guardian now, and there will be expenses to get her and her sister back to my house in Lilongwe."

Mr. Wajiru did not argue. He had told Binti this might happen. He handed the money over to the uncle, who counted it then put it in his pocket. Binti thought of the secret money she had hidden on her, and was glad.

Mr. Wajiru was the last to say goodbye. He gave her a big, big hug. "We won't forget you," he said. The lump in Binti's throat was too big to allow any words to come out.

The next day, Uncle Wysom bundled Binti, Junie, and their belongings into an over-packed minibus, and they headed for Lilongwe.

Chapter Nine

IN SPITE OF BEING UNCOMFORTABLY cramped in, Binti actually slept for most of the trip to Lilongwe. She was vaguely aware of the minibus stopping and starting a few times as people got on and off, but her eyes stayed closed and she fell back to sleep again.

When the bus stopped for the final time, it took Binti a moment to realize everyone was getting off. When someone shoved her to get her going, her body started moving before her mind fully woke up.

"Junie?" she called out. For a terrifying moment, she couldn't see her sister, then felt someone grab her firmly by the arm.

"Come on," Junie grumbled. "Don't just stand there."

At least something was the same. Binti picked up her bag and ran along with Junie.

They couldn't run much. The crowd around the bus station was thick with people and buses. Uncle Wysom didn't speak but, carrying two of their bags, headed off in front of them. Binti was glad Junie had a firm grip on her. They had to rudely push people aside in places in order to keep up with him.

He led them through streets full of shops. Many of the shops were closed because it was Sunday, but merchants sold things along the sidewalk. Old women carried big trays full of bananas on their heads, and small stalls sold vegetables, soap, medicines, and household goods.

They crossed a bridge over a trickle of a river, where people were bathing and spreading fresh laundry on rocks to dry. They left the busy part of the city behind, and walked down roads where houses were behind high walls. Buses, cars, and people on bicycles moved down the road beside them. This part of Lilongwe was quieter than what Binti was used to in Blantyre, and there were no mountains. Finally, they stopped at a small diner.

"Bambo's home! Bambo's home!" Small children ran across the yard and threw their arms around Uncle Wysom. Binti thought her heart would break. Older children, some Binti and Junie's age, spilled out onto the front yard. They stared at Binti and her sister.

A tall, broad-shouldered woman in a flouncey dress came out in the yard, smiling at Uncle Wysom. Her smile froze, then disappeared.

"I had to," was all Uncle Wysom said. "This is your Aunt Agnes," he said to Junie and Binti, then he introduced them to his family.

One little girl came forward to get a closer look.

"You keep away from them," Uncle Wysom told his children. "Their parents died of AIDS. For all we know, these two have it, too. So keep your distance."

"You brought AIDS home to live with us?" Aunt Agnes exclaimed. "How could you?"

"There's no need to worry unless you touch them or drink out of the same cup, things like that," Uncle Wysom told them. "I know all about it."

"That's not right, is it?" Binti whispered to Junie.

"What did you say? I don't like children to be whispering secrets." Aunt Agnes glared at Binti.

"I was saying," Binti began, when Junie didn't speak up, "that neither of us has AIDS, and even if we did—"

"And I don't like children who talk back, either!" Aunt Agnes stood right in front of Binti and Junie, and pointed her finger in their faces. "Understand?"

Junie looked down at her feet. Binti glared back at her aunt for a brief moment longer, then looked away as well. "Yes, Aunt Agnes," she said quietly.

"All right, let's go inside," Uncle Wysom said. "These are my brother's children, so let's make them welcome."

Some welcome, Binti thought.

Aunt Agnes and Uncle Wysom owned and operated a small eating place. Most of their customers were construction workers and truck drivers who dropped by for their midday meal.

"They can help in the restaurant," Uncle Wysom said to his wife. "They are old enough to be useful."

"They can't prepare food!" Aunt Agnes said. "They'll pass on their AIDS."

"They can prepare food for the customers," Uncle Wysom decided. "Keep them away from the family's food."

Binti wondered how her aunt and uncle could be so rude as to say all this right in front of them. Junie didn't say anything.

Binti didn't want her aunt's finger in her face again, but there was something she needed to say. "Junie needs to go to school," she told them, in her most respectful voice. "She is supposed to sit her final exams this year. She took extra classes in Blantyre. She should have extra classes here, too, or at least be in school."

"You have had better schooling than my own children at that fancy school your father sent you to," Uncle Wysom said. "Besides, there is no money for exam fees."

"There's the money you stole from us," Binti said. In the next second, her cheek stung from her uncle's slap.

"Wash your hand," Aunt Agnes said to her husband. She picked up Junie and Binti's bags and headed through the house to one of the bedrooms.

Uncle Wysom's family lived in a few rooms behind the diner. The house was a little bigger than Binti's old one had been, but a lot more people lived in it.

"Is this where we'll be sleeping?" Binti asked. There were three beds in the room, tightly squished together.

"*My* children sleep here," Aunt Agnes said, lifting out one of Junie's dresses. "Look at all these fine things!" she sneered.

"No wonder there was not much money in my brother's business," Uncle Wysom said. "He spent all his money foolishly, on too many nice clothes for his girls."

"They're from the secondhand stalls," Binti said, defending her father. "They didn't look this good when Junie found them. She has an eye for clothes, and she can sew really well."

"Can she, now?" Aunt Agnes said. "Well, she can use her talent to help put food on the table. And don't talk back. I don't want to have to slap you, too. You are just a child, and you are not even my child."

Binti looked to Junie to back her up, but Junie stood like a stone while Aunt Agnes and, soon, the other children, rumbled through the clothes she has worked so hard to fix up.

"What's this?" Aunt Agnes held up the *Youth Times*.

"That's mine," Binti said. "There's an article about me in it."

"Well, aren't *you* important?" Aunt Agnes put it in the pile of things that were *not* going back to Binti and her sister.

"You might as well keep your school uniforms for everyday wear," their aunt said finally. "You don't need all the rest." Binti and Junie were permitted to keep some nightclothes, too, and a dress each for church, although not their best dresses. Binti also got to keep her last "Gogo's Family" script, but only because Aunt Agnes didn't think they could sell it anywhere.

"You can both sleep in the storage room," Uncle Wysom said to Junie. "We'll put a mattress on the floor at nighttime. You'll be comfortable enough."

They were put to work that same day. The diner was closed, because of Sunday, but there were the supper dishes to wash and the kitchen to clean. Binti and her sister were given separate plates, cups, bowls, and cutlery, and told never to use anyone else's.

Binti was glad when it was time to go to bed. The storage room was tacked on to the back of the house. Among the sacks of maize and the tubs of cooking oil, Uncle Wysom put a mattress down for them. Aunt Agnes supplied some old blankets in exchange for Binti's new Chiperoni blankets, which went to the family. They were given an oil lantern, too. "I don't want to see that lantern burning all hours of the night," Uncle Wysom said. "Lamp oil costs money."

At last they were alone. They put on their nightclothes, got into bed, and Junie turned out the light.

Binti missed the noise of their old Blantyre neighborhood. She missed knowing Kwasi was out on the sofa, sleeping or drawing. She missed their father. She missed everything.

"Junie?" she asked. "How long do we have to stay here?"

Junie, curled up, her back to Binti, didn't say anything.

"How long do we have to stay here? Junie!" She poked her sister in the back.

"Leave me alone," Junie told her.

Binti left her alone. She stared into the darkness, listening to her sister cry, until they both fell asleep.

"We must find a good hiding place for our money," Junie said, as soon as Binti woke up the next morning. "Keep your eyes open for one."

There wasn't much time to look. They were kept busy working all day. They did laundry, cleaned out the diner before the lunch crowd came in, and washed dishes. Junie was also given the task of making over hers and Binti's clothes for their cousins.

Before going to sleep on the second night, Binti and Junie looked closely around the storeroom. They found a loose board at the back, and tucked their money in there.

———

A week into their stay, Uncle Wysom made an announcement. "We're going to turn the diner into a bottle shop at night." A bottle shop was a place where people could buy and drink beer and rum or whiskey. "Junie is a good worker—I've been watching her. She can be a waitress and keep the customers happy."

"As long as she's still able to do the work around

the house that I need her to do," Aunt Agnes said.

Binti, who was sweeping the floor in the next room, slammed her broom down. "Junie has to study for her exam! I told you that on the first day we got here. She needs to be in school, and she needs to be studying. She doesn't have time to do all your work."

"Pick up that broom!" Aunt Agnes said. "I'm tired of your complaining. Your sister never complains."

Maybe she should, Binti thought.

"We have taken you and your sister into our home," Uncle Wysom added, "but we are not rich people. We have many children and many obligations. You are family, and we will give you food and shelter. If you want more than that, you should go and find yourselves some rich relatives. Now, go on about your work and stop complaining. You are orphans with no status. Be thankful for what you have."

Binti picked up her broom and went back to work. When no one was looking, she put all the dust under one of the rugs. It wasn't much of a protest, but it was something.

Chapter Ten

THE BOTTLE SHOP OPENED THE NEXT NIGHT. "The evening before July 6, Malawi's National Day," said Uncle Wysom. "People will want to start celebrating early." The last few nights, the storeroom had become even more crowded as he set in a supply of bottles of Kutchie Kutchie beer and cartons of thick Chibuku brew.

Junie was made to work in the drinking place until very late. Binti collected the empty bottles from the table and washed glasses in the back, but she was sent to bed while the bar was still busy.

"I'll need you up early to start cleaning," Aunt Agnes said.

The storeroom was lonely at night without Junie, but the voices and radio music from the bar kept her company. It made the night sound more like Blantyre.

"You're supposed to be out of bed already."

Binti opened her eyes the following morning to see her cousin, Mary, standing over the mattress. Mary was a few years younger than she was.

"I'm coming," Binti replied with a yawn. The bar noise had been comforting last night, but it was also hard to fall asleep to.

"Get up and get my clothes ready for the celebration." The cousins were meeting their classes at the sport stadium to be part of the day's events.

"Get your own clothes ready."

"You're just an orphan. You have to do what I say." Mary kicked Binti's leg through the blanket. "I'm telling Mama you won't get up." Mary kicked her again before running off.

"She shouldn't talk to us like that," Binti muttered. "We're people, too. We weren't always orphans."

"Will you just get up and get to work?" Junie growled. "I was up I don't know how late, and I don't want Aunt Agnes coming in here and screeching. She's liable to forget that she said I could sleep in."

"But they can't—"

"Just go!" Junie pulled the covers over her head.

Binti went.

Because it was Malawi's National Holiday, all the children were home from school. The events at the sports stadium didn't start until the afternoon. The older cousins were supposed to do chores around the house and help with the business, but put more and more of their jobs off on Junie and Binti.

Binti cleaned the diner first, and cleaned up from the family's breakfast before being able to eat her own breakfast of cold nsima and tea.

"Mama said you can have a banana today, too, since it's a holiday," Mary said, coming into the kitchen. She nodded at the bunch on the table. "Go ahead, take one."

Binti didn't wait to be asked again. She tore off a banana and unpeeled it. She was halfway through eating it when Mary yelled, "Mama! Binti stole a banana!"

Binti ate quickly. Soon the banana was solidly in her stomach, and Aunt Agnes could never get it back, no matter how much she screeched.

Junie got out of bed later in the morning to prepare food for the lunch crowd. Binti helped her cut tomatoes and onions for the relish, then washed dishes during the noon rush. She dished out nsima and relish, and chicken and chips, and fetched bottles of Pepsi and Fanta from the storeroom. When lunch was over, she cleaned the diner again so that it would be ready to receive drinking customers in the evening.

One day, one week, passed into another. Binti's school uniform, worn every day to do her work in, soon began to look tattered. She almost forgot that she was ever a school prefect, that she was ever on the radio, and that she ever sauntered through the streets of Blantyre, flashing her script so that people would know she was special.

The older cousins, with the exception of Mary, mostly ignored her except when telling her what to do. The younger ones sometimes used her as a target in their games, tossing maize kernels at her and laughing when she was told by Aunt Agnes to clean them up.

She got back at them sometimes. When no one was looking, she'd take a drink of water from one of their cups and put it back on the shelf without washing it. She hoped to kill off the whole family that way, but as weeks went by with no one dying, she began to lose hope. Plus, with so much work to do all the time, she was usually too tired to fight back.

"Don't stand so close to me," one of the cousins would say, and she'd move.

Junie kept her head down, did her work, and barely said a word. A stain appeared on her school uniform blouse, and she just let it stay there. A button came off, and she didn't replace it. She looked frayed all over.

Junie's silence added to the weight of the sorrow on Binti's chest. At first, Binti wanted to talk about their father and brother, for she ached with misery and longing for them. But Junie refused to talk about them, and, as the silence continued, Binti knew less and less what to say.

In the evenings, when she cleared away the empty bottles, Binti watched Junie serve beers to the customers. The men would joke with her and try to make her laugh. They'd put an arm around her shoulder or waist, and she'd smile while she squirmed away. Even across the dark bar, Binti could see that the smile didn't reach her eyes.

One evening, the bar went quiet, and Uncle Wysom turned up the radio. "Gogo's Family" came on. All the customers were silent, listening to Gogo resolving an argument between two family members, and scolding a villager who had spent all his money on beer, leaving his children without food. Binti remembered that show. Her character had taken food to the drinking man's children, and had told on him to Gogo— more to stir up trouble than out of kindness.

Just as the show's final music faded out, Uncle Wysom announced, "My niece is the girl who plays Kettie on the radio." He gestured at Binti, who was gathering up Kutchie Kutchie bottles.

The customers applauded. Binti, surprised, smiled, and for a moment, she had her own life back.

"Come and sit with me," a customer urged her. "I'll buy you a Malawi shandy. Do you know what that is?" He patted the seat next to him.

Binti climbed onto the stool before her uncle could stop her. It had been a long time since she'd had a treat.

"A Malawi shandy is very good," the man said. "It's ginger ale and juice and—"

"Get off that stool!"

Binti was pulled off the seat, not by her uncle but by her sister.

"My sister is too young to sit in a bar," Junie said to the man. She dragged Binti out of the drinking place and into the kitchen, to the laughter of the customers.

"I wasn't doing anything wrong!" Binti protested.

"You stay away from the customers," Junie ordered. "When you go into the bar, you keep your head down, you gather up the empty bottles, and you get out of there."

"I was only—"

"I don't care. You listen to what I say. If you disobey me in this, you will be in such trouble!"

Binti promised. Junie released her grip on Binti's arm and went back to work.

Binti smiled. Her sister was her old self again. Everything would be all right.

Junie's temper didn't last. She went right back to working silently, and taking whatever the relatives dished out to her. Binti felt different, though. Hearing her old life come back at her jolted her out of the fog she'd been in. All of Malawi listened to her voice! She'd performed on a stage, and people had applauded! Even here, among her horrible relatives, she was still special. She was more than an unwanted cousin, more than just an orphan.

She stopped being so sad and started being angry.

"You're too close to me," Mary told her one morning when they were both in the diner before it opened. "Move farther away."

"You can't tell me what to do," Binti replied, calmly.

"I can so. You're just an orphan. You're nothing. You have to do what I say."

"I'm older, and I don't have to listen to you." Binti deliberately moved closer.

"Get away from me!" Mary yelled. "Your mother died of AIDS!"

"She did not."

"She did, too. And your father. I heard what my father said."

"My mother and father were good people. They didn't go around spreading lies like some people's parents." Binti glared at the younger girl.

Mary squished up her little face until it looked as nasty as could be. "Your parents died of AIDS, and you probably have AIDS, too. Mama says I'm to stay away from you, or you'll give it to me."

"Oh, yeah?" Binti was challenged. "How far away from me do you think you'll have to stay to be safe from AIDS?"

Mary was confused. "Well, at least this far away."

"So if I come a little bit closer, will you be in danger?" Binti took a baby step toward her cousin.

"You better stay back."

"What if I come this close?" She took another step, a bigger one. Mary's eyes widened with fear. "You need to be specific," Binti told her. "I want to make sure I don't come any closer than I'm supposed to. I certainly wouldn't want anything to happen to someone as precious as you."

"Stay away from me."

"And I suppose if I touch you on the arm, you'd catch AIDS for sure."

"Don't you touch me! Mama says you're not supposed to touch me!"

Binti had the younger girl backed into a corner. Mary couldn't get away without brushing up against her.

Binti was enjoying herself, really enjoying herself, for the first time since she took her father to the hospital. She hovered her hand over the little girl's shoulder.

"Mama!" Mary yelled.

Binti brought her hand down on her cousin's shoulder, not hitting her, but firmly enough for her to know she'd been touched. "Is this how I'm not supposed to touch you?"

"Mama! She's touching me!"

"Or how about this? Or this?" Binti touched Mary with the point of her finger, on her arm, her cheek, her shoulder again.

Aunt Agnes was there in a flash. "Get away from her!" Aunt Agnes raised her hand to strike Binti. Binti got herself ready for the blow, but it didn't come. Aunt Agnes's hand remained in the air.

"You're afraid to hit me, aren't you?" Binti realized. "You're afraid that if you hit me, you'll get AIDS." Binti laughed at her aunt's stupidity.

Her aunt looked around and grabbed the fly swatter that was near by. She struck Binti with it, over and over.

The rubber of the fly swatter stung very badly, but Binti was too angry and too proud to let her aunt and cousin see her cry.

I'm more important now than either of you will ever be, she said in her mind to them, while Aunt Agnes hit her and screamed about ungratefulness.

"Can't you just keep quiet?" Junie asked a few minutes later, when Binti was sent out back to help with the family's laundry. Away from her aunt and her cousin, she let the tears roll down her stinging cheeks.

"I was teaching Mary a lesson," she sobbed.

"You weren't teaching her anything," Junie replied. "You were just making things worse."

"How could they be worse?" Binti asked in return. She held up the dress she was washing, blue with lace trimming. Her radio-taping dress that now belonged to Mary. Cold suds ran down her arm, but she kept the dress in front of Junie's face until Junie waved it away. "They took everything from us as soon as we walked in the door."

"You're eating, aren't you? You have a place to sleep, don't you?"

"Why aren't you angrier?" Binti demanded.

"Stop being such a child," Junie said. "You have no idea how I am feeling. Now shut up and work."

Binti dropped the dress back into the suds. "You used to say that it wasn't enough just to be able to eat and have a place to sleep. You used to talk about planning for the future."

Junie kept scrubbing the cousin's clothes. She didn't say anything more.

Chapter Eleven

"ARE YOU SURE THERE WAS NO MONEY left from all those radio shows you did?" Aunt Agnes asked Binti one day. She'd steered clear of Binti since hitting her with the fly swatter.

Binti was scrubbing out the nsima pot. "We had to buy my father a coffin," she replied, keeping her eyes on the pot.

"Yes, I heard about that fancy coffin," her aunt said. "Your father was such an important man then, was he?"

"He was to us," Binti told her, then waited for the lecture about not talking back.

It didn't come, but her aunt didn't go away. She kept standing at Binti's side, watching her scrub.

Binti kept scrubbing the pot, even scratching away at dirt that wasn't there, hoping her aunt would go away.

Finally, her aunt spoke again. In a voice Binti hadn't heard from her before, a voice that was quiet and uncertain and a little sad, her aunt asked, "Do you think my children would do that for me? Do you think they love me so much they would spend all their money on a fancy coffin for me?"

Binti was too surprised by the question to answer it right away. Possible answers jumped into her head, like, Who could love you? and Your children are so awful they'd just dump your body on an anthill.

Instead she turned around, looked directly at her aunt, and said, "Your children would buy you the most expensive coffin they could find."

Her aunt heard Binti's words, then, as if embarrassed by her own tenderness, snapped at Binti to "Face front and get back to work."

I should have told her about the anthill, Binti thought, picturing her aunt being overrun by thousands of little ants. Aunt-eating ants, she thought. It cheered her up.

One night, a little while later, she woke up when Junie came into the storeroom. Aunt Agnes and Uncle Wysom hadn't meant to be kind in separating them from the rest of the family, but they had been. It gave Binti and Junie a chance to be alone with each other.

Junie lit the oil lamp. She motioned to Binti to stay quiet.

Binti watched Junie take some money out of the pocket of her skirt and put it in the hiding place. Then Junie put on her night clothes and crawled into bed beside Binti. She put out the lamp.

"Where did you get the money?" Binti whispered.

"I'm going to get us out of here," Junie whispered back. "We'll find our brother, get a small house somewhere, and finish school. This is not going to be my life."

"But where did you get the money?"

"Men will give you money sometimes if you're nice to them," Junie said. "The nicer you are, the more money they give you."

Binti thought for a moment. "Maybe I should be nice to men, too. We can make money faster that way."

Junie sat up and grabbed Binti so hard it startled the air right out of her lungs.

"I told you to stay away from the customers. If I catch you near them, I'll beat you myself." Junie was so angry, she almost forgot to whisper.

"I'm sorry," Binti said.

"Don't make this worse for me," Junie said, curling away from Binti.

Binti hesitated, then slowly slid her arm around her sister's back. Junie let it stay there as they fell asleep.

Things went on this way for the next two weeks. Most nights, Junie would add money to their secret stash. During the day, the two sisters worked, and Binti, knowing Junie was working on a plan to get them out of there, tried her best not to argue with her aunt and uncle.

"As soon as we have enough money, we can leave," Junie said.

"Then we can go back to Blantyre, and I can get my job back on the radio."

Junie didn't say anything for a long moment. Binti guessed she was thinking of Noel.

"First we'll go to Monkey Bay," Junie said. "We'll pick up our brother. Then we'll decide. We have to live where we can find a place we can afford. Then we can go back to school. We'll still have a chance."

Their chance came crashing down a few days later.

"Mama! Look what I found!"

Mary came running into the diner one morning before she left for school. Binti and Junie had been cleaning for an hour already. Mary clutched a small bundle of bills in her fist.

"Where did you get this money?" Aunt Agnes asked.

"It was in the storage room," Mary declared, "where they sleep." She pointed at Binti and Junie on the word "they".

"It's our money!" Binti shouted. Junie just put down her cloth and sat on the nearest chair. "It's my radio money and ..." Something stopped her from saying anything about Junie getting money from men in the bar.

"And what?" Aung Agnes demanded.

"And that's all. It's my money from the radio show."

103

"You told us there was no more money."

"I lied."

"They probably stole it," Mary said, a nasty little smile on her face.

"Did you steal this money?"

"It's mine," Binti insisted. "I earned it on the radio."

"If you earned it, then tell me how much is here."

Binti opened and closed her mouth, trying to think of what to say. "I don't sit around counting my money."

"I will discuss this with your uncle," Aunt Agnes declared, then left the room to find her husband. Mary left with her, sticking out her tongue at Binti as they went.

Binti sat down beside Junie. They didn't speak.

Uncle Wysom came into the diner soon after, with Aunt Agnes, Mary, and some of the other children.

"You are my brother's children," he said, gravely. "I will not turn you out on the street for stealing from me. I will also not turn you over to the police, although I should. You are in mourning for your father, and when people are in mourning, they can do strange things. But I cannot allow you to remain with my family. You can stay with us for another few days while we find another place for you to go—some family who needs workers. Please stay out of our way until then."

They left the room, taking Binti and Junie's money with them.

Junie and Binti went into the storeroom. They put the mattress down and sat on it. Junie curled up, facing the wall. Binti put her hand on her sister's shoulder. They stayed like that for a long time. They didn't speak, and they didn't cry.

Binti woke up in the middle of the night. The other side of the bed was empty. She moved her hand up and down the blanket, and felt a piece of paper. She struck a match, lit the oil lamp, and read the note her sister left.

Dear Binti: I'm going away to earn money. Don't let them parcel you off to someone else. Go to Mulanje. Find our grandmother. Live with her. I'll come looking for you there. Junie.

Binti got up and got herself dressed. She bundled her few remaining belongings up in the blanket. When the first light showed in the sky, she left the storeroom. She could see well enough to find the cash box, kept behind the bar. She used a knife to pry it open, took out a handful of kwatcha notes, and was away from the diner long before the rest of the household woke up.

Chapter Eleven

ALTHOUGH SHE'D WALKED IT only one time, Binti was able to find her way back to the bus depot. There were not a lot of corners to turn, so she could not make a mistake. The one time she was unsure which way to go, she decided to go in the direction most of the cars, bicycles, and people were going. It was the right one.

Even at that early hour, the depot was crowded with buses and minibuses, with travelers carrying heavy bundles, and with merchants selling fruit and hot tea.

She had no idea how she could find the right bus, but even that problem was solved for her.

"Blantyre!" the driver and ticket sellers called out. "Zomba! Mzuzu!"

"Mulanje?" she asked a driver, in a small, timid voice. The driver waved her in another direction. She followed the point of his arm, but still wasn't sure.

"Mulanje?" she asked again, a bit bolder, then, "Mulanje! I want to go to Mulanje!"

"You are going to Mulanje?" a driver asked.
"Come into my bus."

"How much?"

He named an amount. Binti had a little more than
enough. She climbed aboard.

There was plenty of room on the minibus when
she first got on, but by the time the bus inched its way
through the crowds, vehicles, and roadside vendors,
Binti was squished in beside an old man trying to
read a newspaper and a woman carrying a bundle.
Binti gave a brief thought to her uncle, aunt, and
cousins, then fell asleep. Sometimes, when she woke
up, she was leaning against the old man. Sometimes,
she was leaning against the woman. Neither seemed
to mind. Once, when she woke up, the woman took
some bananas out of her bundle and gave one to
Binti. Binti said thank you, ate the banana, and fell
back asleep.

"We get out here," the old man said kindly. He
had to wait for Binti to get out before he could move.
She shook herself awake and climbed out of the bus.

Binti felt like she had stepped into another world.
Gone were the crowds of Lilongwe, the buildings and
people pressed in on each other. The minibus had
pulled into the petrol station to let people off. Binti
stood with her bundle off to the side, and watched
people being greeted by their families. She saw others
settle down to wait with their belongings—someone
was going to come and meet them, and they had no

worries. Most people just started walking. They had someplace to go.

Binti stood back until the passengers were all dispersed, then she turned and let out a big gasp.

Mount Mulanje rose above the town, rocky and glorious, with patches of mist stuck here and there for decoration. It sat in a cushion of deep green slopes, and rose up all of a sudden, as if it had been wandering and just decided that this would be a good place to stay.

Blantyre had Mount Soche, and it was high, but it was only a hill compared to this.

She stared at it until she heard a car honking its horn, letting her know she was in its way. Then she picked up her bundle, went to the side of the road, looked both ways, and wondered where to go.

Aside from the grocery stores and other little shops in low, cement buildings, the side of the road was covered with street vendors. Binti fingered the money left in her pocket. The ride had been long, and one banana hadn't filled her stomach. She hated to spend money on food, though, when she didn't know what was ahead of her that she might need money for. She kept the money in her pocket, and started walking.

There were a lot of other children on their own. Many were working, selling things, or carrying things on their heads. Others were hanging around, playing some sort of game with each other. Some were laughing, some were begging, some were being chased away by the street vendors.

Binti walked along the side of the two-lane high-way. There were fewer cars there than there had been in Blantyre or Lilongwe, but there were more bicy-cles, most laden down with large bundles of wood or food. One bicycle even had a little goat in a basket.

There were dirt roads running off the paved high-way. Binti looked down one, and saw that other dirt roads ran off it. Gogo could be anywhere.

I'd better ask somebody, she thought, but who?

On top of a bit of a hill, set back from the high-way, Binti saw a church. Her grandmother was a church-going woman. Maybe this was her church. Binti headed for it. As she got closer, she heard singing. She'd forgotten it was Sunday.

The church was full for the morning service. People were singing and dancing in front of the stone benches.

The only light in the church came from small, narrow windows, high up the stone walls. Binti stood at the back, and wondered how she could find out if anyone there knew her grandmother.

She decided to do what her grandmother did—walk up to the front and interrupt the service.

This is just like being at the party at the hotel, she told herself, to give herself courage. She walked quickly, so she'd get to the front before she changed her mind.

The pastor was still singing. Binti stood right in front of him, hoping he'd ask her what she wanted, and hadn't just come up to the front to be blessed.

He bent down to talk to her while the congregation kept singing. "What can I do for you?" he asked. "Is there somebody here with you?"

"I'm looking for my grandmother," Binti said, into his ear. "I came to live with her, but she doesn't know it yet."

"What is your grandmother's name?"

"Precious Phiri."

The preacher straightened up and raised his hand for the congregation to stop singing. He turned Binti around so she faced the crowd.

"This little girl is looking for her grandmother, who lives somewhere in Mulanje. Does anyone know Precious Phiri?"

"I know her," a young man's voice came from the back of the church. He joined them at the front. "And I've met this young lady, too. At your father's funeral. My name is Jeremiah."

Binti remembered. She shook his hand.

"Her grandmother lives four miles from here," Jeremiah told the pastor. "I can take her there after the service."

"Praise God, this young lady will soon be home," the pastor said, and invited Binti and Jeremiah to stay at the front while everyone sang a song of praise and gladness.

When the service was over, Binti thanked the preacher and left the church with Jeremiah.

"You have an older sister, don't you? Is she with you?"

"No, she's not."

"Her name is Junie, isn't it? Is she well?"

"Yes, her name is Junie, and no, I don't think she's well, but I don't know for sure because I don't know where she is."

Jeremiah stopped walking. "What happened?"

Now that she was safe, Binti got angry. "Our grandmother told everyone that our father died of AIDS, and because of that, Junie's boyfriend called off the engagement and our uncle treated us very badly."

"Junie's not engaged anymore?"

"It's all our grandmother's fault. She had to tell everyone that lie."

"It wasn't a lie, Binti. I was with her at the hospital. Your father had AIDS. There was a good chance your mother did, too."

Binti started to cry. "Well, why did she have to go and tell everybody? She ruined everything."

"The truth can hurt sometimes, but lies hurt even more." Jeremiah put his hand on Binti's shoulder. "I don't know what happened with your uncle, but I can imagine. You're here now, and you are most welcome. I'll take you to your grandmother, and you can tell her yourself what happened."

Binti wiped the tears off her face with her hands. She asked Jeremiah in a small voice, "Will Gogo have room for me?"

Jeremiah smiled. "She always has room. Your grandmother is a very important woman. She has a lot of power in this area. You'll see." He led Binti across the churchyard to where his bicycle leaned against a tree.

Binti began to relax. Since her grandmother was so important and powerful, she probably had a nice house, like the Story Time house, and people to help her keep it clean. Maybe Gogo was important enough to get Binti back on the radio.

Maybe I'll even get my own room, Binti thought. Some of the girls at St. Peter's School had their own rooms. Binti had always thought she'd like a room of her own.

"Have you ever ridden on a bicycle before?" he asked.

"No, I never have. Where do I sit?"

"You can sit on my supply box." Jeremiah patted the wooden box strapped to the back.

"What supplies do you have?" Binti asked, hoping it was food.

Jeremiah opened it up. "Condoms, brochures about HIV, blood-testing kits. I'm a peer counsellor. I travel on my bike and talk to other young people—well, any people, actually—about protecting against AIDS, and how to take care of themselves if they have AIDS."

"I thought people just died if they had AIDS." Binti climbed onto the supply box.

"It's true that there is no cure," Jeremiah said. "People in rich countries have AIDS drugs that help a lot, but few people here can afford them. But that doesn't mean we are helpless." Jeremiah got onto the bicycle seat.

"Why did you say 'we'?" Binti asked.

"I am HIV-positive," Jeremiah said. "Now, put your arms around my waist and hang on tight. I'm a good driver, but we'll be going on some very bumpy trails."

Binti, looking at Jeremiah's back, heard the words "HIV-positive" echo in her brain. She also heard, Don't touch my children and Don't drink from our cups. With a bit of hesitation, she put her arms around Jeremiah's waist, not really touching at first, then holding on tightly as Jeremiah started pedalling. He felt as normal as anybody. She soon forgot all about his HIV, and just enjoyed the ride.

They turned off the highway after a very short time, and travelled on dirt roads and then on paths that wove around trees. They passed round clay huts with rooftops made of grass. They rode by lots of children, and lots of chickens who squawked and flew up into the lower branches of the trees. There were times when the ride was smooth, but not many. Binti shrieked and laughed as the bike bounced and shook.

Jeremiah stopped in a clearing. Binti saw a small hut with a grass roof, a few chickens, and lots of children.

"Here we are," he said.

Binti slid off the back of the bike. "There must be some mistake ..." she began. Jeremiah had said Gogo was an important woman. Where was the important house? Who were all these children?

"Your grandmother may be off visiting someone," Jeremiah said. "She really holds the community together."

Just then a small, hunched-over woman came out of the little house. She looked over at Jeremiah and Binti, surprised, then her old face warmed into a huge smile.

"It's Binti!" she exclaimed. In the next instant, Binti was wrapped in her grandmother's arms. "It's my granddaughter."

For better or for worse, Binti was home.

Chapter Twelve

THE OTHER CHILDREN WERE NOT QUITE AS WELCOMING.

"This is your cousin, Binti," Gogo announced. "She's come to live with us."

The toddlers peered out from behind Gogo's skirt, and the older kids continued their game of chase the chicken. Two little girls giggled and whispered together by the fire. Binti counted three babies. Two were lying on a reed mat on the ground. The third was strapped to the back of a hard-faced girl of about her own age, who was stirring a pot of nsima with a large stick. She was dressed in a loose, boy's shirt tucked into a chintje skirt.

"Memory, here, will be glad to have your help," Gogo said.

Binti smiled and held out her hand for the girl to shake. Memory put her stirring stick instead of her hand into Binti's palm.

"You can start by helping with supper," she said, without smiling.

"Tomorrow is soon enough for Binti to get busy,"

Gogo said. Binti took her hand off the stick and wiped it on her bundle, even though it wasn't dirty. "Come and sit with me and tell me about your brother and sister."

Gogo scooped one of the babies off the ground, and nodded for Binti to join her on a low wooden bench outside the hut. One of the toddlers tried to crawl into Binti's lap. He was very dirty, so Binti didn't want to pick him up. Her old school uniform was getting shabby, but as least it was still sort of clean.

The toddler gave up and sat in the dirt at Binti's feet.

"Tell me how you are," Gogo said.

Binti told her everything. She had meant to leave a few things out, like stealing the money for her bus fare, but in the end, she told Gogo everything. It felt good to talk.

"I'm sorry I trusted them to take care of you," Gogo said. "All my good children died young." She was quiet a moment, then asked, "Do you have any money left?"

"No," Binti lied. When Gogo kept looking at her, she reached into her pocket and took out the kwatcha notes that were left.

"Give it to Memory," Gogo said. "We'll put Wysom's money to good use."

Even worse than handing the money over was Memory's smile of triumph. Binti felt like protesting but sensed it would do no good. After all, she *had* stolen the money.

"Maybe there are things in the bundle that we can use, too," Memory said.

"You're not stealing my things!" Binti cried. "Not you, too!"

"Don't get upset," Gogo said. "What Memory was saying is that maybe you have things that you might let us all use, especially if you have extra."

"I don't have anything extra," Binti said, untying her bundle to prove it. "I just have one blanket, one nightdress, and one good dress. Aunt Agnes stole everything else."

"What's that?" Memory asked, pointing.

"That's my script. It's the only one I have left. You're not taking it."

"We're not taking anything from you, Binti," her grandmother said. "These things are yours, and you do what you want with them."

Binti tied the bundle back up, tightly, and put it underneath the bench behind her feet.

By the time they finished talking, the nsima had cooked.

Binti went to the bathroom before she ate. The bathroom was an outhouse on the edge of Gogo's property. There was no place to sit. She had to squat over the hole. She got suddenly afraid that spiders or snakes or even hippos would pop out of the hole to get to her, and she got out of there as quickly as she could. She washed her hands by pouring water on them with a scoop that was floating in a bucket.

Ever since arriving at Gogo's, she'd had a hope in the back of her mind that most of the children belonged to the neighbors. That hope was dashed when the evening meal was served. Even more children showed up. Binti counted thirteen people at the meal. Gogo owned just three plates, so everyone shared. Binti shared a plate with four of the small ones. They all ate with their fingers, something Binti had never done. She tried not to let Memory know she was watching how Memory rolled the nsima into bite-sized balls before dipping it into a relish of boiled leaves. She couldn't see how Memory did it so neatly and easily.

Night had fallen, and they ate beside the dying fire, the coals giving them just enough light to see by.

"In the old days, very long ago, there were no stars in the sky," Gogo said, rocking one of the toddlers in her lap. "It was a girl child who put the stars there. She was on a long journey, and the night was very dark. She built a small fire, then threw the sparks from the fire high up into the sky. They lit up a road for her in the darkness, and that was how we got to have stars." She kissed the sleeping child, and reached over and squeezed Binti's hand.

After everyone finished eating, Memory lit a candle stub and went into the hut. She came out a few minutes later.

"The mats are rolled out," she said, picking up two of the small children and going back inside.

Gogo started to get to her feet but wavered. Binti helped her to stand. "Enough talk for today," Gogo said, and went inside. The other children went with her.

Binti picked up her bundle and stood in the doorway. "Where do I sleep?"

"How about outside?" Memory replied.

"Binti will soon get used to our ways," Gogo said, lying down on a reed mat.

"Choose a spot," Memory directed. "Quickly. This candle has to last."

Binti didn't want to lie down anywhere. There was no empty spot, no place that wasn't already taken up with a filthy child. And there were no blankets.

I'm not sharing mine, she thought. It's mine.

She untied the bundle. The night was chilly, and she didn't want to change into her nightdress with everyone watching her. She'd sleep in her uniform, just for tonight. The blazer would help keep her warm.

She wrapped her nightdress around her church dress to make a pillow, then put them down in the biggest empty space there was, near the door.

"Can we share your blanket?" one of the little girls asked.

Binti pretended to ignore her. Once she started sharing, everything would go and she'd have nothing.

Memory made a disgusted sort of noise, and blew out the candle while Binti was still standing. Binti was plunged into darkness, a deeper, more complete darkness than she'd ever seen before. "Hey!"

"Lie down and go to sleep, Binti," Gogo said. "The morning will be here soon, and you can play with your cousins then."

Binti heard giggling. She hated being laughed at. She wished she were still a prefect and could give them all demerits. She wished she were back in Blantyre, warm in a soft bed, beside her sister.

Afraid to move much for fear of stepping on a child, she dropped to the floor where she was, using her hands to find her makeshift pillow. The children wiggled over to make room for her.

Binti kept changing her position, trying to get comfortable on the hard floor. A mosquito buzzed near her ear. Nearby, she heard teeth chattering, maybe from the cold, maybe from malaria. She tried to ignore the sound so she wouldn't have to do anything about it, but she couldn't. She spread some of the blanket over the children beside her, hoping to keep most of it for herself, but she felt their little hands clutching it and pulling it to them. She let it go, and huddled deeper into her uniform blazer. In a little while, the teeth stopped chattering.

I'll go somewhere else tomorrow, she decided, and that was the last thought in the dark she had that night.

The roosters woke her up. One rooster woke up two roosters, and those roosters woke up all the other roosters. The roosters woke up the dogs. The dogs woke up the mosquitos, and then the birds started singing.

Even if Binti had been able to sleep through all that, she couldn't have slept through Memory.

"Get some water," Memory said, standing over her, holding a pail. "Machozi, show her where the pump is."

"You can't order me around," Binti said. "Gogo said we're the same age."

"Well, start acting like it," Memory said. "We need water."

"Let me wake up first."

"You look awake enough to me."

Machozi was the older of the two little girls who whispered and giggled and never left each other's side. The other girl was called Gracie. Binti thought they were maybe six or seven years old.

"It's not far," Machozi said. "We used to get water from a pond that made everybody sick, but some people from Canada built us a pump."

"Do you know where Canada is?" Gracie asked, her voice almost the same as Machozi's, like two little birds chirping. "Is Canada in Malawi?" "Where are you from?" "Are you a real cousin or a pretend cousin?"

The questions came quickly, from one child then another, faster than Binti could answer. She was four questions behind when she asked, in return, "What are pretend cousins?"

"Pretend cousins are ... pretend cousins."

That explanation didn't tell Binti anything, so she put the question back in her mind to ask Gogo later.

The footpaths wound around patches of woods and other clearings with small huts in them. They all looked the same as Gogo's. Binti knew she'd get lost if she had to come to get water on her own.

"Hurry," Machozi urged. "You don't want to have to wait in line." She skipped ahead, and Binti had to run to catch up with them.

There were a lot of women at the pump ahead of them. Binti got in line behind a woman with a baby on her back. Machozi and Gracie left her there, and scampered away.

"Come back," Binti yelled. "I don't know where I am!"

It was an unfortunate choice of words. "Where do you think you are?" the women asked her, joking. "Where do you want to be?"

Binti glowered and stared at the ground.

"Don't mind us," a woman said. "This is just our way of being friendly."

But Binti was not in the mood. She was hungry and confused, and wanted hot water, soap, and clean clothes.

The women left her alone. She watched them work the pump so that she'd know how to work it when her time came. One by one, the women lifted their pails and tubs of water onto their heads, and walked off down the trails.

Binti filled her pail and headed down the trail she thought lead back to Gogo's. She hadn't walked far before she realized she was hopelessly lost. She put the pail down and started to cry.

"Why don't you put the pail on your head?"

Memory was suddenly in front of her.

Binti wiped her eyes. "That's the old-fashioned way," she said, not wanting to admit she didn't know how.

"Oh, and it's the new, modern way to carry a pail of water in your hands so that your shoulders get sore and half the water spills onto the path." She picked up the pail, propped it on top of her head, using one hand to keep it steady there, and hurried down the path. Binti followed, close behind. She wasn't about to get lost again.

The rest of the day was like that. Memory could do everything better than Binti, including washing the children (in cold water, without soap), washing the plates, and cleaning out the hut. Binti fumbled everything, and Memory was always there, watching and smirking.

She thought she'd had a lot of chores at home. She *knew* she had a lot of chores at Uncle Wysom's. But at Gogo's, there was even more work and all of it was strange and new.

Binti learned a few things that first day. She learned how to find the water pump and find her way home again. Gogo had only one pail, but she had twelve children. Binti fetched so much water that, by the end of the day, Binti was sure she could find the pump in the thick black of night.

Another thing she learned was that Gogo had very little food. "We'll eat tomorrow," Memory told Binti when Binti mentioned she was hungry. "First, we go to school, then we go to the feeding centre. We'll eat there."

Binti cheered up at the thought of school. Maybe she could be a prefect again. If she was a prefect and Memory wasn't, she could order Memory around, at least at school.

"Why is there no food?" she asked Memory.

"Because your father died."

For a moment, Binti didn't understand. Then she did. "You are the cousins!"

She had to sit down. She looked around at all the children, dressed in rags, and at the house made of mud and straw. She felt her stomach grumble with hunger. "But he sent a lot of money!"

"Gogo spread it around. 'Everybody needs to eat,' she'd say. We'd just start to get ahead, then someone else in the neighborhood would die, and the family would need money for the funeral. And so here we are. We can't plan for the future."

"You sound just like Junie," Binti mumbled.

"If it's too tough for you, you can always leave."

Binti heard the hope in Memory's voice. "Don't be silly," she said. "Why would I want to leave?"

The third thing she learned was that Gogo had very definite opinions about some things.

"Gogo, is Memory a real cousin or a pretend cousin?" Binti couldn't tell. She hadn't met all her aunts and uncles, so she didn't know what the children would look like.

Gogo's back had curved in her old age, but Binti could swear she saw the spine straighten as Gogo stared her right in the eye. "There are NO pretend cousins! You are all my grandchildren, and you are all real cousins. Do you understand?"

Binti nodded. "Yes, Grandmother."

She thought about asking Machozi which cousins were real and which were pretend, but Machozi would probably tell Gogo, and Gogo would be furious. It didn't matter. Whether Memory was a real cousin or a pretend cousin, Binti was stuck with her.

Chapter Thirteen

"WE HAVE SCHOOL TWO DAYS A WEEK," Memory told Binti the next day. "We used to have it every day, but our teachers kept dying. The teacher we have now travels around between schools."

"Two days a week isn't much," Binti said.

"For nearly a year we didn't have any school."

Binti despaired at the state of her school uniform. She brushed it off with her hands, but that didn't help much. Not only was it filthy, it was for a school she didn't go to any more. She was worried she'd stand out for not being properly dressed.

"Where's your uniform?" she asked Memory. Memory frowned and looked away.

She must not have a uniform, Binti thought. It was all right for the younger children not to have a uniform, but Memory must find it embarrassing to look different from the others.

But Binti was the only one who looked different. The other students wore their regular clothes. Memory, standing tall in the schoolyard and singing the Malawi national anthem during the flag raising, didn't look embarrassed at all.

After the flag-raising came a prayer for everyone to do well in school that day, then the children split into two groups.

The sun was out, so they held classes outside. The younger kids had their own teacher, and several grandparents helped out. They sat together on rocks they arranged in rows in front of a broken piece of chalkboard.

There were fewer senior students. Binti was considered a senior. They sat on rocks, too, on the other side of the clearing from the juniors, to block out some of the noise from the younger ones reciting their sums and alphabet. There were no books, notebooks, or pens. The teacher drew a diagram of a plant on the piece of blackboard, then had the students find a wildflower and tell each other its parts. Math followed, then an English lesson.

Binti was far ahead of the others in English, as that was the language spoken at St. Peter's. She was surprised, though, that the other students were much faster than she was at fractions. How could that be, when they had no books?

In between classes, there were games and singing, and the senior teacher gave the whole school a lesson on healthy foods to eat. School ended early in the afternoon.

Binti was glad that it was over. The rock was

uncomfortable to sit on. She'd had her own desk at St. Peter's. She didn't like knowing less than the others, and she found it hard to concentrate when she was hungry.

"Get the others," Memory told her. "Make sure we leave no one behind."

Binti still got the names of the little ones confused, but she knew all their faces. They were used to the routine, too, which helped. They gathered around Memory, where she could count them off and make sure everyone was there.

"All right, go," she said. The youngest ones stayed with Memory and Binti. The oldest took off down the path in a race.

After walking for a while, they came to another clearing. Lots of other children were there.

"Where are we?"

"This is the Orphan Club," Memory said. "Are you going to just stand there, or are you going to help so we can eat?"

Memory started walking away. Binti called after her. "Are all these children orphans?" There were as many children in the yard as there had been at St. Peter's.

"Did you think you were the only one?"

There were at least two hundred children in the yard. Binti, too hungry to think about it, followed Memory to see what she could do.

As usual, Memory knew what to do. She wasn't

the only one. Older kids from other schools were also busy, helping the little ones find firewood for the old women, who were cooking big pots of nsima and beans over open fires or organizing singing games. Binti saw Gogo among the women who were looking after the babies and toddlers. Binti watched Memory take the baby off Gogo's back and strap it to her own.

"You, girl, come here and help us," one of the old women called to Binti. Binti was put to work stirring beans. Smoke from the fire kept drifting into her face. This was different from cooking on the stove at her old house.

"Not like that. Put your body into it!" the woman told her, giving her a push forward. The pot of beans was huge, and Binti stirred it with a tall, flat board. "Stir from the shoulder or the beans will burn and the food will be ruined."

Binti tried, but the smoke made her eyes water, and she couldn't do the stirring motion properly, at least not to the old woman's satisfaction. They laughed at her. "This girl has never stirred a pot of beans in her life."

"She has other talents," Gogo appeared at Binti's side. "Off you go, child. Find Memory. She'll get you busy."

"Help us put the mats down," Memory said. Large straw mats were rolled up and stacked against the wall of the half-finished building in the clearing. Binti helped her unroll the mat over the dirt in the yard. Others did the same. The children were very particular about getting the mats straight.

Binti heard a clanging sound. One of the women was banging a stick against an old hubcap that was hung from a tree branch.

All the children rushed to the spot in front of the mats. One of the adults greeted them.

"Hello, boys and girls. Did you all work hard in school today?"

"Yes," the children said.

"That's good, because children who do not go to school cannot come to the Orphan Club. Let's sing a song together—a bright, happy song because this is a bright, happy day."

Binti, standing among the other children, didn't know the words or dance moves to the song, but it was easy to pick up, and she was soon singing along with the rest of them.

After the singing came a prayer, to say thanks for the food they were about to eat, then the older kids helped the younger ones wash their hands at a pump on the edge of the clearing. There was no soap, but the children rubbed the dirt off as best they could in the cold water.

There were almost enough plates to go around. Binti had a plate to herself, and stood in line for her scoop of beans and her scoop of nsima. The clearing went very quiet as the children sat on the mats and concentrated on eating. The food was delicious in

Binti's mouth and felt wonderful in her stomach. When she was finished, she really did feel like singing and dancing.

All the kids washed their own plates, even the small kids, then they gathered for more singing.

"Can we borrow your blazer for our play?" a boy asked Binti.

Binti gathered it tighter around her. "It's mine."

"We'll give it back to you," the boy said. "We're not thieves. We just want to use it for our play."

Binti didn't want to give up anything else. But she had an idea. "You can borrow my blazer if I can be in your play."

"All the good parts are taken," the boy said, "but you can be one of the sisters." He took Binti over to a group of kids huddled together by a tree, planning out the play.

"This is—what's your name?" the boy asked.

"Binti."

"Binti. Let's have the blazer." She took it off and handed it to him.

"Where's the script?" she asked.

"What do you mean?"

"The story—" she began.

"They're waiting for us," a girl said. "There's no time to tell you the whole story."

"You're one of the sisters," the boy said, nudging her in with the other two girls. "Just do what they do."

The group went into the clearing in front of the

waiting crowd. The play was about a mean uncle, played by the boy with the blazer, who took in his brother's children when they were orphaned. He and his family treated the orphans badly. It wasn't exactly like what happened to Binti, but she recognized a lot of things. The play had a happy ending, though. The uncle got AIDS from a prostitute, gave it to his wife, and they both died. In the last bit of the play the orphans had a party in the uncle's house, which now belonged to them.

Binti stuck close to the girls who played her sisters. She hated that she didn't know what was going on and what she was supposed to do. She missed the safety of the script and Mr. Wajiru.

"You haven't acted before, have you?" the boy asked, giving back her blazer.

"I certainly have," Binti replied, "but I've always had a script."

"What's a script?" one of the girls asked.

"It's paper with the words of the play printed on it."

"Anybody can act if they're given the words," the boy said. "But don't worry, you'll do better the next time."

On the way back to Gogo's house, Binti thought about the boy's words. She didn't agree with him—if anybody could do it, why was *she* chosen for the radio show and not the other children who auditioned? She tried to come up with things she could say to him to put him in his place the next time she saw him. Then she remembered how awkward she'd felt during the play and how comfortable the other kids seemed, making the play up as they went along. Maybe there were things she could learn, after all.

She thought about it some more while she helped get the little ones ready for bed, and kept thinking about it as she fell asleep. She didn't even notice that her blanket was being used to keep five small children warm in the night.

Chapter Fourteen

BIT BY BIT, THE STRANGENESS OF LIVING with Gogo and the cousins began to wear off. Binti got up as soon as the first rooster crowed, and was busy all day. She was usually tired by the time the darkness came. She fell asleep easier if she was tired.

The early part of the night wasn't so bad because she could hear others moving around her, trying to settle down. The hardest time was if she woke up in the middle of the night, when everyone was asleep and still. That's when she felt the most lonely. She'd try to hear her father straining to breathe in the next room, or her brother's pencil sketching something by candlelight in the living room. She'd want to hog all the covers—if she had covers—so Junie would wake up and snarl at her. But there was no Bambo, Kwasi, or Junie.

The cousins took some sorting out. They changed all the time. Sometimes there were four babies, sometimes only one. Some days, one toddler left and was soon replaced with another.

"Gogo looks after children when their own mamas are too sick to do it," Memory told her. She was pounding maize kernels with a thick stick into a hollowed-out log.

"So they're *not* all real cousins, then."

"Are any of these children not good enough to be your cousin?" Memory asked, giving the maize some extra-hard pounds.

"Don't be so touchy," Binti said. She nodded toward the baby that was strapped, as always, to Memory's back. "When does he go back to *his* mother?"

Memory slammed the stick so hard into the maize it bounced right out again and sent the maize spilling into the dirt. "The baby is a *she*! You didn't even know that. You don't even know her name." She left Binti to take care of the mess.

Binti shooed away the chickens that were already pecking around the spilled maize. She picked the family's food up out of the dirt, then picked up the pounding stick, which was almost as tall as she was. Her arms soon ached from the work of crushing the hard corn. Being angry and hungry helped her finish the job.

There was just enough maize for one meal for all of them. When the kernels had been crushed, Binti put them into a wooden winnowing basket, and sifted it all down to flour. She spread the flour out on a cloth on the ground to dry. She got Machozi and Gracie to keep the chickens away from it. She felt proud of herself for doing all that work without any help—or criticism—from Memory.

Binti went for a pail of water. When she got back, she saw Memory sitting on the bench outside the hut with Gogo beside her. Memory was nursing the baby.

Binti didn't know what to think. "How can you do that?" Binti stammered. "I mean, I thought you had to be a mother before you could ..."

"This is my daughter," Memory said.

Binti's jaw dropped. She sat down on the bench next to Memory.

"Gogo said I should tell you. She said you needed to know, but I don't care if you know or not." Memory's words were defiant, but she looked down at the dirt.

"Memory was living with her uncle—not one of *my* children, praise the Lord. Her uncle's friend had AIDS. Memory had never gone with anyone, so this man thought he'd be cured if he made her go with him."

Binti didn't understand. "Go with him where?"

"He made her go with him as if she was his wife."

It took Binti a moment, and then she understood. It made her want to throw up.

"He didn't get cured," Memory said. "He still has the AIDS. He gave it to me, and he gave me this baby."

Binti couldn't look at her. Memory was *her* age.

"When I came here, I wanted to forget everything,

but Gogo wouldn't let me. She said I should change my name to Memory, so that every day I remember will be a curse to that man. She says the curse will be stronger if I live and be well."

"It doesn't help to hide things," Gogo said. "Secrets make our shame bigger. Memory has nothing to feel shame about. She is a good girl, and a good mother."

Binti couldn't imagine having a baby. Thoughts and questions spun in her head. In the end, though, to her surprise, there was only one question that seemed to need an answer right away.

"What's her name?" Binti asked.

"Her name is Beauty," Memory said.

Beauty was put into Binti's arms. She'd never held a baby before. The tiny girl yawned, her face relaxed and beautiful. She looked like Memory.

Some of the toddlers finished their playing and crawled up onto Gogo and Memory's laps. One of them leaned against Binti. They all sat on the bench together and watched the afternoon slip away.

Chapter Fifteen

"HOW ARE YOU SETTLING IN?" Jeremiah asked Binti. He was visiting Gogo as he did his rounds of AIDS educating.

Binti thought about his question. Life was hard at Gogo's, but it was hard for everyone, not just for her because she was an orphan. She'd had more food and had been cleaner at Uncle Wysom's, but she hadn't been happier. Here, she was hungry often and cold at night, and her school uniform was embedded with the red dust of Malawi, but her grandmother loved her, and the work she did was for people she cared about.

"I'm settling in fine," she said.

"Is there anything you need?"

"We need soap and blankets and food and some books to read and more clothes for the children." She counted things off on her fingers as she listed them.

Jeremiah laughed. "You and everyone else up here."

Two of the little boys ran up to Jeremiah. "You said you'd bring us one!"

"I brought four," he said. He reached into his wooden box and got out four blue plastic shopping bags, the kind Binti would get when she bought things in the market back in Blantyre. "I had three for you, then I found another one, just today."

The boys were too excited to say thank you. They grabbed the bags and ran off.

"What do they need bags for?" Binti asked.

"You'll see. Listen, why don't you try to earn some money? Then you can buy some of the things you need."

"You mean go out to work? Is there a radio house near here?"

"I don't think there's one of those, but keep your eyes open. Maybe you'll think of something. Is there anything else?"

"I need to find my brother and sister," she said. "But that's probably too much to ask."

"Not necessarily," Jeremiah said. "I'm connected to AIDS support groups around the country. Maybe we can find them." He took out a pen and a note pad. "What are their names?"

Binti told him. "My brother is up at Monkey Bay with our uncle who runs a fishing business. I don't know where Junie is." She stepped closer to Jeremiah and looked around to be sure no one was able to overhear. "Before she left Lilongwe, she was making money for us by being nice to men. She said she was going to go off and make enough money for us to live together." Binti hesitated. "Maybe she's being nice to men again, you know, for money. Do you have any idea where she might do that?"

Jeremiah thought. "I don't, but other people might. I'll see what I can find out." He put his notebook away.

"Jeremiah?" Binti hestitated. What she wanted to ask was personal and awkward. "Does Memory have AIDS?"

"She is HIV-positive, which means that she has the virus that leads to AIDS."

"And her baby?"

"Beauty is also HIV-positive. She may have gotten it when she was born, or she may have gotten it from Memory's milk. Your grandmother wanted me to test them, and Memory agreed."

"Will they die?"

Jeremiah leaned against his bicycle. "Babies who are HIV-positive don't usually live very long in Malawi, although they do in countries that have the right drugs. But miracles can happen. People, even in Malawi, can live for a long time with HIV if they have a good diet and people who love them."

"What should I do?"

"You won't catch it from living with them."

"No, I mean, what should I do ... for them?"

Jeremiah smiled. "Be their family, and let them be yours."

He got on his bike and was about to pedal away to

his next stop when a whole flock of little boys ran, laughing, into the yard. They were playing soccer. Binti wondered where they got the ball, then realized that the ball was the shopping bags, wound up tightly.

"They've been collecting bags for ages," Jeremiah said, before saying goodbye.

Binti sat down to watch the game. She kept players from getting too close to the nsima flour, spread out in the yard to dry.

Jeremiah did an AIDS presentation at the Orphan Club the next day, and stayed to watch Binti and some of the other children put on a play. This time, they used Binti's script. Binti played Gogo. She'd tried to get everyone to memorize their lines, reading them over and over to those who couldn't read, but the cast still said things that came into their head as the play went on. Binti had so much fun playing Gogo, she didn't worry about the rest.

"We have a surprise for you, Binti," Gogo said one evening. Neighbors came into Gogo's yard, bringing sticks of wood to build up the fire. "It's a treat for all of us."

"All right, quiet down now. It's time." Someone brought out a wind-up radio, the kind that didn't need batteries, turned it on, and the group around the fire got quiet.

The opening music for "Gogo's Family" came on. Binti wanted to cry. She listened with the others, remembering her times in the studio, remembering how it felt to be so special, how much she'd loved hearing the director say, over and over, "Talk like real people!"

"That's my Binti, talking on the radio," Gogo said. People applauded. They wanted to know how she could be on the radio and sitting with them in Mulanje at the same time.

"Tell us the story of being on the radio," the neighbors urged.

Binti felt shy at first but soon warmed up to it as people laughed and clapped. She even mimicked the director telling the cast they needed to do it again.

For a time after that, people referred to Binti as "The Girl on the Radio." There was another radio show the next week, and they asked Binti to tell her story again. She made it a little different, pretending to be one of the cast members trying hard not to sneeze during the taping. Binti saw even Memory laugh at that one.

Most of the people in the village had never been away from Mulanje. Many had never even been away from the village. Binti thought about what it would be like to be them, listening to stories from her.

She felt like the old Binti.

Then, the very next week, when everyone was gathered around the fire, another girl's voice came out of the radio. Another girl was playing the part of Kettie. Binti was officially off the radio.

"That's not your voice," someone said. "The radio girl is saying she's Kettie, but you're supposed to be Kettie."

"When I had to leave Blantyre, they hired someone else to play Kettie," Binti said, trying not to show that she minded.

"And we are much happier to have her here with us than far away on the radio," Gogo said.

The group listened to the radio play. Binti kept sitting with them. She wanted to get up and run away, but she didn't want it to matter that much. Although she tried not to listen, she found herself involved in the story. Sometimes she thought that she would say a line better than this new girl, but then the story would take over again.

When it ended, the people around the fire seemed just as happy with the show as they were when Binti was in it.

There's nothing left, Binti thought. There's nothing left of me.

Gogo had been whispering to some of the children. They got to their feet.

"We want to put on a play," they announced.

The play was about Binti. Memory played Binti. She was on the radio, then her father died and she was sent to live with a cruel uncle. Then, finally, she came to Mulanje, and everyone was happy. The play ended, and the people around the fire clapped.

Binti clapped, too. She knew they were being kind. She knew Memory wasn't making fun of her. Memory still treated her with scorn sometimes because Binti was all thumbs at doing the things that mattered, such as starting a fire or cooking nsima. But she didn't dislike Binti. Binti clapped because they were being kind, and she wanted to thank them.

But even as she clapped, she could feel herself slipping away. She'd lost her mother, her father, her home, her school, her brother, and her sister. And now the only thing left that made her feel special, that kept her from being just another orphan on the mountain, was gone.

There's nothing left of me, she thought again.

It was a feeling she could not shake.

Binti moved through the next few weeks in a fog. She did the work Gogo needed her to do to keep the cousins cared for. She sat in classes two days a week, and stood in line at the Orphan Club for her plate of nsima and beans. But the light inside her had gone out.

"Sometimes you can feel better if you do good deeds," Gogo said to her one day. Binti tried it. With the help of one of the neighbors, she turned her nightdress into clothes for Beauty. There was enough material in her good dress to make a skirt for Machozi and a blouse for Gracie. Binti was not good at sewing—most of the work was done by the neighbor—but she did feel good presenting her gifts. The fog lifted for a little while.

One day, there was great excitement at the

Orphan Club. There was a party in the clearing with
many of the villagers and guests who collected money
for the Club from overseas. Some local boys had
formed a rock band, with drums made of oil cans, a
guitar, and a harmonica. They played, and people
danced and clapped.

The children had practiced special songs and
plays for the day, and they performed these for the
guests.

After the plays were over and everybody had eaten,
the guests made a very exciting announcement. They
were going to give out soap!

Binti joined the line of children waiting their turn.
The lucky ones at the front of the line were laughing
and jumping, holding their precious gift. Binti got
hers, a solid pink bar that smelled good and clean.
She looked down at her shabby, filthy, St. Peter's uniform. Soon it would be clean again.

"I have some news for you." Binti looked up to see
Jeremiah at her side. He led her away from the noise
of the soap line. "We've found your brother."

Binti looked around. "Where? Is he here?"

"We'll take you to him. It will take a few days to
arrange, though."

"Why a few days? Why can't we go today? Where
is he?"

Jeremiah put his hands on Binti's shoulders.
"Binti, your brother is in jail."

Chapter Sixteen

IT WAS ALMOST A WEEK BEFORE Jeremiah's friends were able to arrange permission for Binti to visit the prison. She rode on Jeremiah's bicycle back to the main highway in Mulanje, where they caught a minibus to Blantyre. Jeremiah had money from the AIDS organization to pay for their fares.

In Blantyre, they went to the office of Jeremiah's friends, who drove Binti and Jeremiah to the prison.

They were taken through two sets of high, barbed-wire fences surrounding an area with many buildings. In the fields, hoeing the vegetables, were prisoners in white shirts. Binti looked for her brother, but she didn't see him there.

It wasn't a regular visiting day, so the guards directed them to the warden's office.

"You have just learned that your brother is here," the warden said. He was a friendly man who spoke in kind tones. "He is being held with other boys his age, separate from the adults. We are taking as good care of him as we can." The warden turned to Jeremiah.

146

"Of course, there is no money to spend on prisoners. I can't pretend that life is easy in my prison. We do what we can, especially for the younger ones, but it is not enough."

"Can I see my brother now?"

They were taken through two sets of fences and asked to wait in the social worker's office. This small wooden shack with a tin roof had its own fenced yard. Binti was too excited to sit in the office. She went out in the yard to wait. From there she could see the huts for the women prisoners. Some of the women were sitting on the grass outside. Binti waved, shyly. Some of the women waved back.

And then her brother was there.

Binti threw her arms around him almost before seeing him. She could feel that he was even skinnier than before. He was crying, too, just like she was.

"Come in and sit down," Jeremiah urged.

Binti and Kwasi went into the hut. It was crowded with supplies and prisoners' belongings being stored. They sat on old crates, too numbed to talk for a while.

"Kwasi is here because he has been charged with theft," the social worker said. "He will tell you the details when he is able to. For now, I will just tell you that his uncle accused him of stealing food from his store, and called the police."

"Has he been to trial yet?" Jeremiah asked.

"Oh, no, he won't be going to trial for some time

yet. Some boys are here for years before they go into a courtroom."

"Come on," Binti said, her hand on her brother's arm. She stood up. "We're going back to Gogo's. We're leaving now."

Binti and Kwasi got to the door. Jeremiah stopped them.

"It's not that easy, Binti. Maybe we can get him out, but it won't happen today. Come back and sit down, and we'll talk about it."

They went back in and talked. Kwasi told them what had happened.

"I didn't mind all the work," Kwasi said. "I knew my life would not be as good as it was, but I couldn't get used to being so hungry. The family had food, but they wouldn't share it with me." Binti guessed he hadn't been allowed to draw, either.

"Gogo said that all of her good children died young," Binti said.

"Their grandmother is a formidable woman," Jeremiah said. "We can bring her in to help on this. What do we need to do to bring this boy home to his sister?"

"Get the uncle to drop the charges," the social worker said. "This is such a common thing. The child loses his parents, they get in with people who do not care about them, and they end up here. We have so many boys here who have lost one or both of their parents."

Jeremiah talked with the social worker about his organization coming into the prison to do AIDS education with the prisoners and the guards. While they were talking, Binti told Kwasi about Junie, and about life with Gogo. "What is it like for you here?" she asked.

"I have a couple of friends," he said. "We stick together and keep away from the others as much as possible."

"Where do you sleep?"

"We all live in a building that's just one big room. We sleep on the floor. It's very crowded. We all have to sleep on our sides because there's not enough room to sleep on our backs."

"Do you get enough to eat?"

"We are all supposed to get nsima and beans once a day, but the guards just bring in big pots of food. We have to fight to get to it. Sometimes we get lucky, though. One of my friends has family that bring him fruit, and he shares it with us."

"Can we go get some food for Kwasi?" Binti asked, interrupting the men's conversation.

The social worker said they could leave it with the guards at the gate. They would get it to him, and he would deliver it to Kwasi. "After this, you can come on visiting days and bring food with you."

It was hard to say goodbye. Binti had no idea how she'd get money to buy her brother extra food, or even come and visit him again, but she promised to do both things.

"Don't give up hope," Jeremiah said. "Now that we know where you are, we'll be back."

Binti watched her brother be taken back through the prison gates. She knew why he didn't look back and wave. He didn't want to end up crying in front of the other boys.

They went to the market, got some fruit, and dropped it off at the gate. The guards had been alerted, and promised to take it to the social worker.

After that, Binti thought about asking to go visit her old friends at the Story Time house, but decided not to. That was her old life. She had a new life now.

Chapter Seventeen

"I AM *DONE* WITH MY CHILDREN!" Gogo fumed. "The ones who made me proud are dead. The ones who are left are not fit to be children of mine!"

She went from neighbor to neighbor, looking for bits of money that would help her get to Monkey Bay. The neighbors who could help, did. She left the next day.

"I know you will take care of the little ones," she said to Memory and Binti as she left. "I'll be back soon."

A neighbor woman was going with her. Binti and Memory watched them head down the path.

"She's not really well enough to make this trip," Memory said.

"Gogo is sick? I know she's old, but I didn't know that she's sick."

"She worries a lot. It's not good for her."

They kept looking down the path where Gogo had gone.

"Is your brother going to make more or less work?" Memory asked.

"What do you mean?"

"I mean, will he help out, or will he want to be looked after?"

Binti smiled. "No worries about Kwasi. You'll see."

"At last, you're smiling."

"What does that mean?"

"You've been moping around here for weeks, as though you were the only one who's lost something."

Binti didn't like that. "I do my share of the work."

Memory retied the chintje that held Beauty to her back. "Yes, you work" she replied, "but you still don't act like you're one of us. Not really. You act like you've been stuck here by accident and you're waiting for someone to fish you out. Like you're special."

"Well, I was special, once."

"Oh, yes, the radio. That will be what you tell people all your life, 'I was once on the radio.' "

"What do you know about it?" Binti demanded. "You don't know what it's like to have something so wonderful, and then lose it."

"So why not be happy for what you had? Really, Binti, sometimes you don't make any sense."

Binti got annoyed at Memory for saying that, then got even more annoyed because Memory was right.

The next morning, Binti woke with a dull pain in her belly. The throb in her head wasn't helped by the rooster who insisted on coming right into the hut to announce morning's arrival. Binti got to her feet and chased him outside.

"Your leg is bleeding," Gracie said, as she raced Machozi to the outhouse.

Binti looked down. There *was* blood on her leg. She couldn't find a cut, so that could mean only one thing.

"I've got the AIDS! I've got the AIDS!"

Memory was at her side in a flash, but as Binti jumped up and down in a panic, Memory just looked at her and laughed.

"Didn't your mother ever tell you about the monthlies?"

Binti stared at her for a long moment, then looked down at her legs, the panic ebbing away. "My sister told me."

"Go get washed. I'll get you something. And you two—shoo!" she said to the two little girls giggling nearby.

"Use these cloths," Memory told her, when Binti was clean.

"Don't you need them?"

"I don't have the monthlies as long as I'm feeding Beauty." She touched the soft, faded cloth. "This was my mother's dress," she said.

Binti understood fully what a gift she was being given. She took the prefect pin off her uniform blouse and fastened it to Memory's shirt. It was the best thing she could think of to give her.

Gogo expected to be back in a couple of days, but she was gone for almost a week. The children were lonely without her. Binti and Memory could manage all the work that needed to be done—they usually did most of it, anyway. But it wasn't the same without Gogo, who could calm a crying baby or quiet an argument between Binti and Memory and make them both feel like winners.

Having an adult around who loved them made all the difference.

Gogo returned late in the afternoon of the sixth day. Kwasi was with her.

It was like one of those miracles the pastor was always saying could happen but that Binti had never seen. She looked up from the cookfire, and there he was. He seemed taller than he had been in prison, and he was thin, of course, but he was still grinning his lop-sided grin that made him look like he knew all the weird, funny secrets of the world.

"Kwasi!"

Binti clung to him until Gogo told her to let him sit down.

He sat on their bench beside their grandmother, and was soon swamped by the overflow of children who wanted to be near Gogo. Binti sat down beside her brother.

Memory walked into the yard, a full pail of water on her head.

"That's our cousin, Memory," Binti said. "The baby on her back is her daughter, Beauty."

Kwasi got up. With a toddler in one arm, he reached up and took the pail of water off Memory's head with the other. A bit of water splashed out onto Memory's face. To Binti's surprise, she didn't seem to mind.

There wasn't much talking that night. Gogo was tired and Kwasi was overwhelmed. It was hard to fit everyone into the little hut, but Kwasi said it was still less crowded than the prison had been.

Binti slept well that night. Her brother was with her. They'd find Junie and bring her home, too. Gogo would make room for all of them.

The cool, dry weather of the winter moved into the spring. Soon, the hot, wet summer months of December and January would arrive.

"There's not much food here," Binti said, apologetically, to Kwasi.

"There's more than I had at the prison," he told her, "and here I don't have to fight anyone for it." Bit by bit, he regained his strength. On days when the Orphan Club didn't meet, and there was no school, he hiked into Mulanje Town to look for work. Sometimes, he brought back food that he'd earned. On other days, he was paid in money.

"I wish I could earn money, too," Binti said to Memory. "There are so many things we need. If we had another pail, then two people could go for water at one time, and cut down the number of trips."

"The roof needs to be repaired, too," Memory

said. "The rains can be very heavy here. I've heard of families being crushed when their roofs cave in. But you're needed here."

Binti knew what Memory was saying. Several of the toddlers were sick, Gogo spent almost all of her time lying down, and even Memory had days when she was just too tired to pound the nsima.

Binti saw the tiredness come on Memory all of a sudden one day. Memory's face turned the color of ash, and she lay right down in the dirt where she had been standing. Binti ran to her, but Kwasi got there first. He took off his shirt and put it under her head for a pillow. Then he untied the chinje holding Beauty and tied it around himself, with Beauty in the front. He made silly cooing noises at the baby, and didn't seem to mind at all that he looked silly.

Malawi's hunger season came, and the price of maize went up. Machozi and Gracie showed Binti and Kwasi how to look for roots and other bush foods to stretch their meals with. Machozi's and Gracie's hunger made them quieter. They didn't chirp as much.

Sometimes Binti would catch Kwasi drawing in the dirt with a stick. She knew his fingers were hungry for the feel of a pencil against paper.

She had an idea. She fetched her radio script. "Draw on the back of this," she said.

"Are you sure?"

"It's paper. I don't have a pencil, though."

"Don't worry. I'll find something." Kwasi's whole body started to glow with excitement. He got a charred bit of wood from the fire pit. Right away, he started to draw—birds, first, of course, but as the little ones gathered around to watch him, he switched to drawing their faces.

That's one problem solved, Binti thought.

Jeremiah kept looking for Junie. He contacted all the AIDS education organizations he knew, and asked them to look for her as well.

"It's very kind of you to do this for us," Kwasi said, when Jeremiah stopped in to see everyone and report on his progress. "I know our sister will appreciate it when you find her."

"Oh, no, no, it's OK, no need to ..." Jeremiah stammered and he looked all around the yard—everywhere but at Binti and Kwasi.

"He's in love with our sister," Kwasi said, after Jeremiah had left.

"In love with Junie? But he only met her at Bambo's funeral."

"What does that matter?"

Binti remembered when she'd met Jeremiah at the church in Mulanje. He had asked a lot of questions about Junie.

Then she had another thought. "But he is HIV-positive."

"So? HIV affects the blood. It doesn't affect the heart." Kwasi looked across the yard at Memory, caught Binti watching him, and switched his attention to the pattern of the bark on a nearby tree.

"Oh, for heaven's sake. Am I the only normal person here?" She started to walk away, then had still another thought. "Hey—can you imagine Junie riding on the back of Jeremiah's bicycle?"

Kwasi immediately got out the script, and with a stick from the fire pit, using just a few lines, drew a very prim-looking Junie perched on the supply box while Jeremiah worked the pedals. She looked very Junie-ish, back straight, high-buttoned blouse, no-nonsense expression on her face. It was very funny, and it made Binti miss her sister even more.

A few weeks later, there was one less toddler to feed.

He hadn't been with them very long. His own mother had died just the week before.

"I didn't know he was so sick," Binti said, looking at the little boy's face as Kwasi held the body in his arms.

"Children can die of broken hearts, just like adults," Gogo said. "He missed his mother, and his sadness allowed the thing inside him that was not well take over him. We must gather reeds to bury him." People without money for a coffin or a blanket to bury someone in would weave a cover of reeds to wrap up the body.

"Let's build a coffin," Binti said.

"How? We have no lumber or tools."

"We'll find something."

Gogo stayed in the hut with the boy's body, while Kwasi and Binti planned and built a coffin.

With Machozi and Gracie, they searched out sticks and reeds. They tried weaving the sticks together, but that didn't work. Then they tied the sticks with reeds, but that still wasn't very secure. Finally, Binti borrowed a machete to notch some of the bigger sticks, then tied reeds around the joints to make them tighter. That held together.

"This wouldn't work for a heavier grownup ..." Kwasi said, "but it will hold a small child." He used a piece of coal to draw a small bird in the bottom.

There was no formal funeral with a pastor. The neighbors gathered and buried the boy beside his mother in an informal graveyard among some trees. They sang songs and prayed and read from the Bible, and sent the little boy off to heaven the best way they knew how.

Chapter Eighteen

Two days later, Binti was trying to bathe a small, squirming child. A man came into the yard, his eye cast down. Memory was washing clothes.

"This is your little brother?" he asked.

"My cousin," Binti said. The man talked quietly to the little boy to hold his attention while Binti finished washing him. Finally, the child was dressed.

"My son is a little smaller than this one," the man said. "He will be gone soon. Can you build him a coffin? I want to bury him with dignity, but I have no money."

"Can you help us repair our roof?" Memory asked, wringing out a shirt and hanging it over a branch to dry.

The man stepped back to get a better view of the house. "I'm not an expert," he said, "but I'll do what I can."

"Then we'll build your son a coffin," Memory said.

"I would have done it for free," Binti told her later. "He looked so sad."

"He'd still be sad, and our roof would still have holes," Memory told her. "You build the coffins. I'll talk to the customers."

And, just like that, the children were in the coffin business. Over the next few days, Memory took orders for three more baby coffins. Each coffin they made was different, because the shape of the sticks they used was different. But they all held together, and gave the babies in them a better resting place in the dark ground.

One neighbor paid in yams. The other two gave them cash. The children met with Gogo to decide how to spend it.

"I know you will want to give this money away," Memory said to their grandmother, "but if we buy lumber and tools, we can use it to make more money."

"If we get an extra pail, we'll have to go to the pump less often," suggested Binti.

"I have smart grandchildren," Gogo said. "I'll let you decide."

In the end, lumber and tools won. Kwasi voted with Memory, which was no surprise. Binti took care of Beauty and the other little ones while Kwasi and Memory walked to Mulanje Town to see if there were any secondhand tools they could buy.

Binti tried to tie Beauty to her back, the way Memory did, but all she managed to do was make a fool of herself in front of Machozi and Gracie. She looked to Gogo for help, but Gogo was laughing so hard she was doubled over. Binti tried to be offended, but it was much more fun to just laugh with them.

"I have the smartest grandchildren, and the funniest," Gogo said, when she was able to catch her breath. She helped Binti tie Beauty to her back with the chintje, then went into the hut to take a nap.

Binti enjoyed being in charge for the afternoon.

"We need water," she said to Machozi and Gracie, and the little girls ran off with the pail. She got the nsima ready to cook, swept the yard, and when the girls came back with the water, she sent them to look for firewood. Much of the time, Beauty slept, warm and solid against Binti's back. Later, Binti felt her squirming. She got the girls to help her take off the chintje sling, gave Beauty a bath, and sat with her, stirring the evening meal over the small cook fire.

"We're back!" Kwasi called out, as he and Memory walked into the yard. They were carrying several long pieces of lumber. On top of the boards was an old hammer, a rusty handsaw, and a small bag of nails.

"Kwasi drew the owner's picture, and he gave us this wood," Memory said.

"Memory bargained for the other things," Kwasi said. "You should have heard her. We even have some money left!"

They put the boards down, and shooed the little ones away from the tools.

Binti got them each some water to drink. "Supper

is almost ready. Go wake up Gogo," she said to Machozi and Gracie.

"Gogo! Gogo!" The girls scampered into the hut.

"We should make a sign," Memory said, "to let people know what we're doing. And we should have a name for our business."

"Heaven Shop Coffins," Kwasi announced.

"Our coffins will take you swiftly to Heaven," added Binti.

"Heaven Shop—sounds like a lucky name," Memory said, in agreement.

"Gogo! Wake up!" they heard Gracie laugh.

"Do you think we should use a piece of one of the boards to make a sign?" Binti wondered.

"Gogo! Gogo! Wake up!" Gracie wasn't laughing this time.

Kwasi was the first into the hut, but only because his legs were the longest.

The two little girls were pulling on Gogo's arms. "Get up!"

Binti and Kwasi took the girls outside. Memory came out a few minutes later, tears flowing down her face.

"She's gone," Memory cried. "Our Gogo is gone."

———

They made her a coffin.

Kwasi touched the saw to the lumber but couldn't

bring himself to make a cut. He handed it over to Binti. "You were always better at it than I was."

Binti made some practice cuts, then closed her eyes and imagined her father there beside her, telling her what to do. The joints she cut fit together, and although she had to use many more nails than her father would have, the coffin held steady.

There wasn't quite enough lumber to complete the lid, so they attached a woven reed mat to cover the bare places. Machozi and Gracis collected the reeds. Memory wove them. Kwasi didn't have any paint, so he used a nail to carve a bird in the bottom of the coffin. They lifted Gogo in and made her as comfortable as possible.

Jeremiah came to be with them.

"Will the relatives come and take our things away?" Binti asked, looking around the small yard. There wasn't much to take.

"They won't be coming," Jeremiah told them. "Gogo told the pastor to call them if anything happened to her, and to tell them to stay away. She said they've hurt you, and should not be given the chance to do it again. She also had the pastor make a document saying that her things come to you, not to her children."

A lot of people came to Gogo's funeral. There were so many deaths in the area, people had to pick and choose which funerals they went to, or they would never get anything else done. It showed Binti how well-loved her grandmother was, that so many people came to say goodbye. They cried for a woman they had loved and who had loved them. They sang the funeral songs, and prayed. They hugged the children and brought food to the house, if they had any to share.

The pastor was full of emotion. He raised his hands to heaven as he spoke. "This good woman did the work of ten people here on earth. The love she showed her children can be seen in this magnificent coffin they built for her so she could have a peaceful rest now that her work is done. We can help her to help them by going to them for the coffins we need, and by all being family to one another."

The cemetery in the churchyard was crowded with graves and with mourners. Binti and the other children dropped the first handfuls of dirt on the coffin. She and Kwasi helped the toddlers toss in their handfuls. Memory was crying too hard. The dirt landed with a soft thud against the coffin they'd made.

As they left the churchyard, several people approached them to order coffins for members of their families who were too ill to recover.

"I'll come and see you in a few days," one man said. "You'll want some time to be sad before you start to work."

"Don't let us be sad for too long," Kwasi told him. "We have a lot of children to feed."

Chapter Nineteen

GOGO'S HOUSE, FILLED WITH CHILDREN, felt incredibly empty. The little ones, used to Gogo's comforting, clung to Binti, Kwasi, and Memory.

Jeremiah stayed with them for a few days, then had to leave. "I'll ask around again. Maybe someone has seen Junie," he said as he headed out.

"She should be here," Kwasi said.

"I think so, too," Jeremiah agreed, and he pedalled away down the path.

The coffin business grew slowly, but it grew.

Memory talked to the pastor and the Orphan Club people, and got a small loan to buy lumber and more tools. She talked a shop owner into giving her an old tin of paint that was almost empty. There was just enough paint in it for Kwasi to paint a sign. He shredded the end of a stick to make a brush. The sign read

HEAVEN SHOP COFFINS
Our Coffins Will Take You Swiftly to Heaven

Machozi and Gracie, too young to use the tools, kept the yard swept. "We must show respect for those who are grieving," Binti told them. "A tidy yard shows that we take their grief seriously. It also cuts down the risk of fire." She had learned well from her father.

They made money. Not a lot, but enough to eat on the days when the Orphan Club did not meet. Missing Gogo didn't hurt so much when they kept busy.

"We'll need to build another hut some day," Kwasi said. "When the little ones start to grow, there won't be enough room for all of us in here."

"Maybe we could even buy blankets before the winter comes," Binti suggested. To be warm in the chiperoni would be a wonderful luxury.

Kwasi did most of the talking with customers, although if there was a dispute over costs, Memory stepped in. He was so friendly, it was easy for people to like him. He took walks around the village and told people about the Heaven Shop.

Not all the customers wanted coffins. One woman wanted a bench so she could sit outside her house when her work was done. Someone else was tired of sleeping on the floor, and wanted a bed. Kwasi drew pictures of how they should be built. Binti did most of the building, since she was the best at measuring. Her arms were strong from carrying water and children, and her skill had grown since Bambo's funeral. Memory argued with suppliers, getting the best possible price for lumber.

Some customers paid with money. Some paid with food. One customer paid with a box of fancy soaps his wife had been sent from her cousin in England. She'd never used them, and now it was too late. Memory traded the fancy soaps for some plain ones, and for an extra pail for fetching water.

"The rain will be here soon," Memory said. "We'll need a way to keep the lumber dry."

"And to keep *me* dry when I work with the lumber," Binti said.

"The lumber is more important," Memory said, with a grin. Binti grinned back.

Jeremiah helped them rig up a roof of plastic sheeting over the work area. Binti could stand under it in the heavy rain and stay dry. She usually had a lot of small children under there with her, playing with the sawdust and small pieces of wood.

The next time Jeremiah came, he had news.

"I've found your sister!"

Binti called for Kwasi, who was playing soccer with the younger boys. Memory came out of the hut where she'd been sweeping.

"She's not very far from here," Jeremiah said. "She's living in Muloza, right on the border with Mozambique, about twenty miles from here."

"Why didn't you bring her back with you?" Binti asked.

"She doesn't want to come, not yet. Let's sit and talk."

They gathered around the fire pit. Memory handed him some water.

"What's Junie doing in Muloza?" Kwasi asked.

"She shares a small house with several other women. They entertain the truck drivers and, well, that's how they earn their money."

Kwasi jumped up and knocked the cup of water from Jeremiah's hand. "Liar!"

"Kwasi!" Binti grabbed hold of her brother, but he shook her off and pulled Jeremiah to his feet by the front of his shirt.

"You can't say things like that about our sister!"

Jeremiah didn't struggle away, and he didn't fight back. He seemed very calm as Kwasi glared hard at him. Then Kwasi let him go, sat back down, and started to cry.

Jeremiah crouched beside him. "Your sister Junie is one of the finest women I've ever met," he said quietly.

Kwasi wiped his eyes on his sleeve. "Junie *can't* be doing that. You don't know her. She would never do that."

Binti remembered their life in Lilongwe. "Junie got lost," she said. "I know what that's like, to feel yourself slip away."

Kwasi thought about this, than he slowly nodded. "That happened to me in Monkey Bay. I started to forget who I was, what made up me. It was even worse in prison."

"I lost my self when my uncle's friend used me," Memory said. "Gogo helped me get myself back."

"And when I was told I was HIV-positive, I thought that the disease was all I was. There was no more Jeremiah, there was just the HIV."

"How did you get your self back?" Kwasi asked.

"I met other HIV-positive people. They said they weren't sick, they were living positively. As soon as I heard that, I felt Jeremiah coming back into me."

There was quiet for a moment, as they all thought about their lives, then Kwasi stood up.

"Get yourself ready, Binti," he said. "We're going to get our sister."

"You can't!" Jeremiah said. "She's ashamed. She needs to be treated gently, and . . . and there's more."

"What?"

"She wanted me to tell you. Men pay more if she doesn't make them use a condom. She asked me to test her. She's HIV-positive."

"So?" Kwasi asked.

"She doesn't know if you'll want her back this way."

"She thinks she's so special," Binti said. "I'm tired of waiting for her." She hurried off to get ready.

"But you don't know where she is," Jeremiah protested.

"Which is why you'll have to come with us," Kwasi told him.

Getting ready took no time. As they were leaving,

Kwasi turned to Memory. "Is this all right with you?"

"Bring your sister back," Memory said. "We need her here. And hurry. We have orders to fill."

Binti, Kwasi, and Jeremiah headed down to the highway. Jeremiah grumbled until Binti said, "Don't you want to see her again?" and then he brightened right up.

They got a ride on the back of a tea truck, with children who had been working on the tea plantations. Binti sat on a sack of tea leaves as the truck sped down the highway.

In a very short time, they were in Muloza. Binti looked across the border at Mozambique. It looked the same as Malawi. The truck driver let them out at the side of the road.

"Where do we go now?" Kwasi asked Jeremiah.

"This way." A neighborhood of small houses spread out behind the highway bottle shops. Some homes had women and children sitting out front. Trucks of all sizes were scattered around the town.

"This is her house," Jeremiah said. It looked the same as all the others, small and shabby, but the dirt yard had been freshly swept, and there were some flowers growing along the side.

"This looks like Junie's place," Kwasi said.

He went up to the door. It opened up just as he was raising his hand to knock.

Binti didn't recognize the woman in the doorway.

"We're looking for our sister, Junie Phiri," Kwasi said.

The woman smiled. "Junie talks about you all the time. Hello, Jeremiah." She showed them into the small living room, where a few other women and their children were spending time together before the night's work began.

And then there was Junie.

Kwasi was hugging her before Binti even realized her sister was in the room. When he finally released her, Binti was able to get a good look at her.

Junie wore a kerchief around her head, a skirt shorter than their father would have allowed, and a pink top, the sort the old Junie would have tossed aside in disdain if she found it in the secondhand pile.

Binti kept looking, but made no move toward her. Junie, too, stayed where she was.

When Binti finally said something, it wasn't at all what she expected to say.

"You just left me there!" she blurted out.

"I thought it was the best thing to do."

"You could have taken me with you!" Binti started to cry, great choking sobs. She tried to stop them, but they kept coming.

Junie took a clean, neatly-folded handkerchief out of the pocket of her too-high skirt, and gently dried the tears that rolled down Binti's cheeks until Binti was able to stop crying. She smoothed out the collar on Binti's old school uniform blouse.

"Where's your prefect pin?" she asked, gently.

"I gave it to Memory," Binti said.

"For you to give away something so precious ... you're not a child anymore, are you?"

Binti leaned in to whisper another bit of news she had. Junie kissed her on the forehead. "I think you're taller, too," Junie said.

"Do you know about Gogo?" Binti asked.

"Jeremiah told me."

"Get your things," Kwasi said. "We're going home."

"I'll help you pack," Binti offered.

The other women laughed. "Junie's been packed to join you ever since she got here."

"It won't take long, then," Kwasi said.

"Wait a minute," Junie said. "You can't just barge in here and tell me what to do."

"Yes, we can," Kwasi said.

"And hurry up," Binti said, "or you will be in such trouble."

That did it. Now it was Junie's turn to cry and cling to her sister.

"Oh, no, you've made her cry," Jeremiah said. "That's not right."

The women laughed at Jeremiah's obvious infatuation. "Never mind," one of the women said, putting her arm around his shoulders, "if Junie doesn't want you, I'll marry you."

Junie became so embarrassed that the only way out of it was for her to get busy barking orders to everyone about where her things were, and how they should be careful when carrying them.

One of the women in the house went out and found one of the truck drivers who was heading to Mulanje. In a very few minutes, the bundles were loaded in the back. Junie said goodbye to her friends.

"Please come and visit us in Mulanje," Binti invited them, and they said that they would.

Soon they were back on the highway, headed out of town.

Binti sat beside her sister. Junie had changed clothes. She was wearing her old school uniform again, but it had been repaired and cleaned.

"I've been saving it for this day," Junie said, when she saw Binti looking at it. "I'm sorry that you saw me the other way."

"This looks more like you," Binti said.

"It *is* me," said Junie.

Binti moved closer to her big sister. Soon, they'd be home.

Chapter Twenty

"HERE WE ARE," BINTI SAID.

Gogo's place was now home to her, and she thought the Heaven Shop looked very professional, but she tried to see it through Junie's eyes. Would Junie think the house was too shabby, the workshop too rough? Would she turn around and leave?

But Junie was smiling. And when Memory came out of the house to greet them, Junie's smile grew even bigger.

"You're Memory, of course," Junie said. "Jeremiah's told me all about you. And this must be Beauty."

"And Gogo told me all about you," Memory replied. "You are welcome, and you are needed."

"What's in the bundles?" Gracie asked.

Junie gave Beauty a kiss on the forehead. "There's something for everyone. I've been collecting things for a long time. I was planning to come here in two weeks, at Christmas, as a surprise."

"We surprised you instead," said Kwasi. "Give

175

Junie some space," he told the little kids who were crowding around, excited.

In the first bundle was soap, needles and thread, a cook pot, some plastic plates, and a plastic basin perfect for giving the little ones a bath. Another bundle held secondhand clothes and blankets. In the third bundle, smaller and heavier than the others, was rice, tea, dried beans, and a few medical things. The fourth bundle was the most exciting.

There were balls for the younger ones, paper and colored pencils for Kwasi, a new piece of chintje for Memory, and a book of plays for Binti.

"It's from a secondhand bookseller," Junie said. "You were so good in the radio show. You should keep practicing, and be an actor when you grow up."

Binti hadn't realized how much she missed having something to read until she held a book in her hand again. *A Book of Plays for Young Actors*. Binti read the English words from the cover. "Not many people here understand English," she said.

"You'll have to translate, then," Junie told her. She had notebooks and pens in her bag, too. She started talking with Kwasi and Memory about what they should do with the money she'd brought with her.

Binti, eager to get inside her new book, started walking away to find a quiet spot.

"I have one more thing for you, Binti." Junie handed her a copy of the *Youth Times*, the one with the article about Binti in it.

"How did you ... did you get it back from Aunt Agnes?"

"No. I think they burned the one they took from you. Someone was selling these in the street. I knew you'd like to have it again. It's something to be proud of."

Binti sat under a tree and opened the newspaper. Inside was the photo of her, standing in front of the microphone, reading her script. But the girl in the photo was almost a stranger to the girl under the tree. Had she really marched around town showing off her script? Binti felt a twinge of embarrassment at her old self, at what had seemed important to her then.

But it *was* something to be proud of, that she had been on the radio and had done a good job. She remembered the letters she got, and the times Mr. Wajiru had praised her, and how her father called her, "My famous daughter."

And now she had other things to be proud of. She had stood up to Aunt Agnes, even though it meant a beating. She could carry water and cook nsima and look after the small children who needed her. And she was learning to really act, to actually become a character in a play, not just do what the director told her to do.

Binti looked up from the photo of her old self. Across the yard, the older ones were talking and planning under the Heaven Shop sign, and the younger ones were screeching and laughing like it was already Christmas. In a dry corner of the yard, several coffins, large and small, were stacked neatly, waiting for customers to pick them up.

"Tears go into our coffins," her father once said, after broken-hearted parents had picked out a coffin for their child. "Tears make the coffins lighter and make the dead rise faster to Heaven. It's harder to go to Heaven if no one cries when you die. There is a lot of good sorrow in our coffins."

Since then, Binti had cried for her father and for her grandmother. There were almost certainly more tears to come, because life and love seemed to require tears from her, just as they required hard work and hard times, and keeping on when she wanted to give up.

Her father had been right. There was sorrow, but there was laughter, too, and belonging, and being needed and wanted.

Binti got up from the ground and brushed herself off. There was water to fetch and food to prepare. By the time the others were tired of planning, she'd have supper ready. They would eat together and go to sleep. And tomorrow, they would all make it through another day.

THE END

Author's Note

HIV stands for Human Immune-deficiency Virus. This virus destroys the body's immune system, the system that helps us recover from illness. People whose blood has been tested and is found to contain HIV are said to be HIV-positive.

AIDS stands for Acquired Immune Deficiency Syndrome. People with AIDS have first become infected with HIV, which has weakened their immune system. People with AIDS don't have the strength to fight off other illnesses. It is these other illnesses that cause the death of people with AIDS—illnesses such as tuberculosis, pneumonia, or even an ordinary cold.

HIV is spread through unprotected sex, sharing unsterilized needles or razor blades, or, in the days before donor blood was tested, through contaminated blood. HIV-positive mothers can pass the virus on to their babies during pregnancy, childbirth, or while breastfeeding. HIV cannot be spread through kissing, touching, or sharing cups and dishes.

Although it cannot be spread through casual close contact, fear and lack of education lead to the shunning of people with HIV. Not long ago, in the United States, parents tried to keep a little boy from attending school with their children because he had contracted HIV through a contaminated blood transfusion. Such behavior adds to

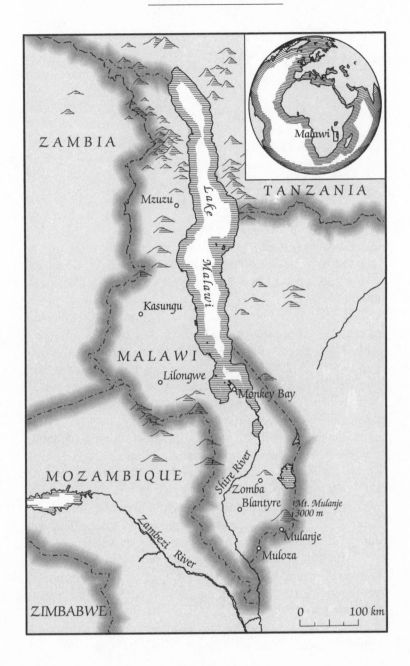

the problem by increasing the shame associated with AIDS; and shame prevents people from seeking and sharing the truth about AIDS.

Forty million people around the world today are living with HIV/AIDS, and the number is growing. Here is a breakdown of that forty million:

- just over 20 million are women
- over 3 million are children under the age of 15
- 15 million live in Sub-Saharan Africa

More than thirteen million children in Sub-Saharan Africa have lost their parents to AIDS. The number of these "AIDS orphans" is expected to double by 2010.

Unlike other mass diseases, such as influenza, AIDS usually takes people when they are young adults, at their strongest and most economically productive. This is causing huge difficulties for countries with already-stretched resources, because medical personnel, civil servants, and teachers are dying faster than they can be replaced. Drugs that slow down the virus (they do not kill it) are available, but they are expensive. In southern Africa, for example, they cost more per month than most people earn in a whole year. Cheaper drugs have been promised, but they are slow in arriving.

War spreads AIDS when women are raped or forced into prostitution, when governments spend health care and education dollars on weapons and soldiers. Poverty spreads AIDS when people's education is cut short and their choices are reduced, when the cost of medicine is beyond their reach, and when even such basic self-care as good nutrition is difficult or impossible. We may not have a cure for AIDS and HIV—yet. But we can take action to prevent war and alleviate poverty.

Deborah Ellis

About the Author

DEBORAH ELLIS was born in Northern Ontario but grew up farther south, in Paris, Ontario, Canada. Like many writers through history, she was a creative loner as a child, at odds with formal education in her youth, and a voracious reader at all times. As an adult, Deborah has been occupied with many issues of interest to women, such as peace, education, and equality in society at home and abroad. She works at a group home for women in Toronto, Ontario, reading and writing in her spare time.

Deborah also travels whenever she can, listening to people's stories, especially the stories children tell about their lives. Whether it is Parvana having to invent herself as a new character in her own story, or Henri being amazed by another character's story and enriching his own because of it, the children Deborah writes about really live on the page. Their vividness teaches us something about how real children and young people, in other times or in other places, might have lived or do live now, with whatever life gives them to bear.

Following are some questions you might like to hear Deborah Ellis answer about her work, about *The Heaven Shop*, and about her life. If you would like more information, check out the Canadian Review of Materials Web site for an excellent profile by Dave Jenkinson: http://www.umanitoba.ca/outreach/cm/profiles/ellis.html

Q: Why did you choose to write about AIDS orphans?

A: We have created a world where most children live in some form of war, and I write about them to try to do honor to their strength and courage. When we see stories on the news of refugees, war victims, and kids affected by AIDS, we see them as a mass of people. It's hard to remember that they are individuals just like us, with families and hopes and fears just like we would have in that situation. In my books, I try to show how alike we are, even if the circumstances of our lives are very different. My hope is that, the more we know about other people, the less likely we are to stand by and watch them suffer.

Q: Where did you do your research for *The Heaven Shop?*

A: I spent time in Malawi and Zambia, meeting with kids affected by AIDS, and with the adults who care for them.

Q: In *A Company of Fools*, you wrote about children during the time of the Bubonic Plague in France in the Middle Ages. Do you see any parallels between that time and AIDS in the present day?

A: There are some differences, of course, since we have progressed a lot since then in our knowledge of science and disease, and how to live healthy lives. There are, unfortunately, a lot of similarities, too. We are fearful of what we don't understand, and this fear has made us treat people with HIV/AIDS with disgust, discriminating against them, and making them feel like outcasts. This is medieval thinking, and it's disappointing that, in these ways, the human race has not moved forward as far as it should have.

Q: You write a lot about calamities. Why does this interest you so much?

A: Courage interests me—when we have it, when we don't, and how we make the decision to be brave or cowardly. Calamities provide a good background to explore courage. I've written about children in Afghanistan, in refugee camps in Pakistan, and caught up in the ongoing war in Israel and Palestine—places where children are forced to be braver than they should ever have to be. In our day-to-day lives as well, in ways big and small, we all have to make the choice to have courage or not. As an anti-war activist, I want to write about how people act as decent human beings in situations designed to kill off all that is good within them. Kindness is all around us, even in times of despair.

Q: Is Binti a real child?

A: Binti is a made-up character, going through a lot of things that kids in her situation are going through. She was inspired by a little girl I met who played a character on a radio soap opera that deals with social issues.

Q: You have a sister—do you identify most with Binti, the younger sister, or Junie, the older one?

A: There were two children in my family, and I'm the youngest. My sister Carolyn is almost two years older than me. We fought when we were kids, but get along great now. She's an incredible woman—a nurse, musician, and mother of two strong girls, Kim and Deanna.

Q: Are you going to write more books about the orphans of Africa?

A: I am working on a non-fiction book about kids affected by HIV/AIDS in Sub-Saharan Africa, which will contain interviews with kids talking about what has happened to them, how they feel about it, and how this affects how they see themselves and the world.

Q: What is the most important lesson you have learned from your time in Malawi and Zambia, and the other places you've been to?

A: I have learned that there is no such thing as "other people's children." The world's children are a blessing to all of us. They are also our responsibility.

Q: How long are you going to keep writing?

A: Until I fall over.